FORBIDDEN DOORS

the haunting

BILL MYERS

Tyndale House Publishers, Inc.   Wheaton, Illinois

ISBN 0-8423-3991-4

Printed in the United States of America

07 06 05 04 03 02 01
7   6   5   4   3   2

To Lynn Marzulli,
for his help,
encouragement, and
steadfast faith.

So use every piece of God's armor to resist the enemy whenever he attacks, and when it is all over, you will still be standing up. But to do this, you will need the strong belt of truth and the breastplate of God's approval. Wear shoes that are able to speed you on as you preach the Good News of peace with God. In every battle you will need faith as your shield to stop the fiery arrows aimed at you by Satan. And you will need the helmet of salvation and the sword of the Spirit—which is the Word of God.

Ephesians 6:13-17

1

1:36 A.M. WEDNESDAY

The cloaked figure stood outside the house. Slowly, reluctantly, she started to climb the porch stairs. At the top she reached for the doorbell, then hesitated.

"No," she whispered, her voice hoarse and pleading. "It is too late, it is—"

Suddenly she convulsed, doubling over

as though someone had punched her in the gut. She leaned against the wall, gasping. Carefully, almost defiantly, she rose. She was a handsome woman, in her late fifties. Strands of salt-and-pepper hair poked out from under her hood. There was a distinct air of sophistication about her, though her face was filled with pain . . . and fear.

Another convulsion hit. Harder, more painful.

She rose again. More slowly, less steadily. This time she would obey.

She stretched her thin, trembling hand toward the doorbell and pressed it. There was no response. She tried again. Nothing. The doorbell didn't work. Not surprising in this neighborhood.

She opened the screen door, which groaned in protest, then rapped on the door.

Knock-knock-knock-knock.

Rebecca was the first to hear it. She stirred slightly in bed, thinking it was still part of a dream.

The knocking repeated itself, louder, more urgent.

Her eyes opened.

Knock-knock-knock-knock.

She threw off her covers, then staggered out of bed and into the hallway. Scotty's door was shut. No surprise there. He was the world's soundest sleeper (that's the beauty of not having a care in the world). She glanced toward Mom's room, then remembered. Her mother was off at a funeral of some third aunt twice removed.

"I'll only be gone three days," she'd assured them. "I've asked that nice Susan Murdock from church to check in on you. You think you'll be OK for three days?"

Seventeen-year-old Becka and her fifteen-year-old brother figured they'd be OK for three weeks, let alone three days. They tried their best to convince Mom that they didn't need some semistranger from church checking up on them. Of course, it hadn't worked.

"Well, I'll have her drop by, just in case," Mom had said.

Becka reached the stairs and started down, hanging on to the banister for support. The cast had only been off her leg a few days, and she was still a little shaky. Then there was Muttly, her pup. His bouncing and leaping around her feet didn't help.

"Muttly, get down," she whispered. "Get down."

Knock-knock-knock-knock.

Becka reached the bottom of the stairs and crossed to the front door. She snapped on the porch light and looked through the peephole. An older, frail woman stood there. Becka hesitated. The visitor certainly looked harmless enough. And there was something very sad and frightened in her eyes.

Knock-knock-knock—

Becka unbolted the door and opened it. It stuck slightly, and she had to give it an extra yank. But even then she only opened it a crack.

"Rebecca Williams?"

"Yes."

"I am sorry to bother you at this time of evening, but there is someone . . ." She trailed off, pulling her cloak tighter as if fighting off a chill. "There is someone who needs your help."

Becka fidgeted, eying the woman carefully.

"Please," the woman insisted. "If I may come in for just a moment? It is most urgent."

Becka's mind raced. The woman hardly looked like a robber or a mugger. If worse came to worst, Becka could always scream and bring Scotty running downstairs. Besides, she couldn't shake the image of those eyes: tired, sad, frightened. It was against her better judgment, but—

Becka opened the door. The woman nodded a grateful thank-you and stepped into the entry hall. "You won't regret this, I assure you. My name is—" She broke off at the sound of a harsh little growl.

Becka looked down. Muttly had his hackles up and was doing his best imitation of being ferocious. "Muttly!" she scolded. "Stop that!"

The puppy growled again until Becka reached down and gave him a little thwack on the nose. He looked up at her and whined feebly.

"I'm sorry," Becka said as she turned back to the woman. "That's not like him at all. He's usually so friendly."

"It does not surprise me," the woman answered, keeping a wary eye on the animal. "I am afraid he senses it, too."

"Senses it?" Becka asked. Normally she would have invited the stranger to have a seat, but at 1:30 in the morning the woman had a little more explaining to do. "What exactly does my dog sense?"

The woman pulled back her hood and shook out her hair. It fell past her shoulders, long and beautiful. She extended her hand. "My name is Priscilla Bantini. We have not met officially, but we have many friends in common. I am the owner of the Ascension Bookshop."

Becka sucked in her breath. The Ascension Lady! The woman who owned the New Age bookstore, who made the charms for

5

her friends . . . who sponsored the kids in
the Society. Becka swallowed hard. She
wasn't sure how to respond.

The woman watched her carefully. "I
know what you must think; however, I assure
you I had nothing to do with the pranks the
children have been playing on you."

Pranks! Becka thought. *I almost get hit by a
train, and then I'm kidnapped by satanists. Some
pranks!*

The woman continued. "Someone desperately needs our help. They have been calling
upon me, begging for my assistance, but I
have neither the strength nor the power."

"I'm sorry. . . ." Becka shook her head.
"What are you talking about?"

"Someone needs help."

"What's that got to do with me?"

"You have the strength and the power
they need."

Becka blinked. "What?"

The woman spoke calmly and evenly. "As
a Christian, as a disciple of Christ, you have
both the strength and the power to help this
. . . person."

Becka closed her eyes a moment. She'd
heard the Ascension Lady was weird—but
she didn't know she was a total fruitcake.
"You're going to have to run that past me
again," she said.

"There is a spirit—the soul of a deceased human—that is trapped in a mansion across town. It desperately wants to be free, to reach its resting place, but it cannot do so on its own. It needs your help."

Becka scowled. "I'm not sure what you're—"

"I know you disapprove of the source of my power, but this poor creature needs to be set free. Together you and I can—"

"What creature are you talking about?"

"The one inhabiting the Hawthorne Mansion across town. It is the spirit of a human, a victim of a tragic murder, that is trapped there by negative energy. It desperately wants to be free." The woman's voice grew more urgent, her eyes more pleading. "The anniversary of its death will be here in just three days, and it is begging me, pleading with me to seek your help."

Becka shook her head. "I still don't understand. How am I supposed to be able to help?"

"According to my charts, the anniversary of the murder is in conjunction with a unique alignment of planets. This Friday, April 21, is when the spirit can make its escape. This is when we can join forces— bringing it forth in a séance and helping it reach its eternal resting—"

Suddenly a voice boomed, *"What are you doing here?"*

Becka and the woman spun around to see Scotty, Becka's younger brother, towering above them on the stairway. Although he was only a ninth grader, his height and position above them gave him a commanding presence.

Priscilla cleared her throat. "You must be Scott Williams. My name is—"

"I know exactly who you are." He started down the steps toward her.

Priscilla forced a smile. "Yes, well, I was just telling your sister that—"

"No one invited you here."

Becka looked on, shocked at her brother's manners. "Scotty."

He continued down the stairs toward the woman, and there was no missing his anger. "Haven't you caused us enough trouble?"

Priscilla backed half a step toward the door. "I am not here to cause trouble. I am here to help. According to my astrological charts—"

"I don't give a rip about your astrological charts." He reached the bottom of the steps, but he didn't stop. He walked directly, purposefully, toward her.

"Scotty!" Rebecca exclaimed.

He turned toward Becka. "This woman brings in that channeler creep, nearly gets you killed, helps those cruds who snatched you, and you expect me to be polite?"

Before Becka could answer, Scott turned back to Priscilla. "Get out of here."

The Ascension Lady reached behind her, fumbling for the door handle.

"Scotty—"

"Get out."

The woman pulled the door open and backed outside. "I apologize for the intrusion. I was expecting more Christian love, but I can certainly understand." She stumbled over the threshold as she backed out onto the porch.

Scott continued toward her. "Get off our property before I throw you off."

"I did not come for myself."

Scott reached for the door.

"As I told Becka, the spirit of a deceased human desperately needs our—"

He slammed the door shut.

Becka stood in the silence, staring at her little brother. She was both shocked and a bit in awe. Then, for the first time, she noticed he was trembling.

He turned to her. "They won't hurt you again," he said, his voice quivering. "I promise you, Sis. I won't let them hurt you again."

~

2:45 A.M. An hour later Scott lay in his bed, staring at the ceiling. No way would he be able to get back to sleep. Not after tonight. He was too steamed. How *dare* the Ascension Lady show up at their door. How dare she ask for a favor. After all her people had done to them? No way!

As for that cheap line she threw in about "Christian love" . . . give me a break!

Normally Scott was pretty much a happy-go-lucky guy. "Live and let live," "Be everybody's bud"—those were his mottoes. And if things ever got too tense, there were always his wisecracks. But there were no jokes tonight. And for good reason.

He turned on his side, his thoughts still broiling. They had moved to this town three months ago, after Dad had died. And for three months, he and Mom and Beck had been constantly hassled by the Society and all their hocus-pocus.

Why? Why did those creeps have to keep bothering them? Weren't he and Mom and Becka the good guys? Why were they always the ones put on the defensive?

He knew Beck wouldn't fall for the woman's line about helping some deceased spirit. Becka's heart might be soft, but her brain wasn't. Still, there had to be some way to stop these guys from their constant harassment. Better yet, there had to be some way to get even.

To get even . . . His eyes lit up with interest. Now there was an idea.

But even as he thought it, a still, small voice whispered that he might be stepping out-of-bounds—that getting even wasn't exactly the right plan of attack.

Scott ignored the voice. Enough was enough, and he and Becka had had enough. Again the thought of evening the score tugged at him. He toyed with calling Z, his mysterious friend on the computer bulletin board. Maybe Z would know of some weakness in the Society that Scotty could use against them. But he already knew what Z's response would be. He'd heard it before. He'd even used it before: "These people are not your enemy; they're only prisoners of your enemy."

Yeah, right. Well, prisoners or not, Scott was going to find a way to protect his sister. And it being the middle of Spring Break, he'd have plenty of time to think of something.

◡

11:50 A.M. Becka turned from the front seat of the car to her friends. "You sure this is the right house?"

"Oh yeah." Julie, one of her best pals—a super jock with perfect clothes and a figure to match—grinned at her. "Everyone in town knows this place, right, guys?"

The others agreed: Ryan, the driver with the killer smile; Krissi, the airhead beauty; and Krissi's part-time boyfriend and full-time intellectual, Philip.

When Rebecca had called Julie to tell her about the visit from the Ascension Lady and the invitation to participate in a séance, Julie thought it would be fun to grab the rest of the guys and go for a drive. So here they were, driving up a steep hill and slowly approaching the Hawthorne Mansion.

Becka looked out her window. For a haunted house, it was a little disappointing. She'd expected something covered in weeds, unpainted, and overflowing with cobwebs and banging shutters. Granted, the place was two-and-a-half stories high and had pitched roofs sloping every which direction, but instead of looking like a home for the Addams Family, it looked more like it belonged to the Brady Bunch.

As if reading her thoughts, Julie explained. "They pay a gardener and housekeeper to keep it spruced up, just in case someone ever wants to buy it."

"It's been vacant all these years?" Becka asked.

Philip answered. "My dad's a real estate

agent. They get offers all the time, but they always fall through."

Krissi giggled, "Right after they spend a few minutes alone in there."

"You're going to help, aren't you?" Julie asked. "You know, take part in that séance?"

"You're going to a séance?" Krissi asked nervously.

Philip joined in. "Hey, maybe we can all go."

The others responded, "Yeah, neat, cool." Nearly everyone was excited. After all Rebecca had been through, attending a séance was not at the top of her "Things I Gotta Do" list. Ryan, on the other hand, was silent and noncommittal.

"Pull over here," Philip said, pointing to the curb. "Let Becka get out and take a look."

Ryan brought his white Mustang to a stop directly across the street from the mansion. Everyone piled out except Krissi.

"Aren't you coming?" Philip asked.

"I'm not feeling so great. I think I'll sit this one out."

"Come on," Philip insisted. The others joined in until Krissi finally gave in. "All right, all right," she whined as she crawled out of the car, "but if we die, you're all going to live to regret it."

No one was quite sure what she meant, but that was nothing unusual when it came to Krissi.

As they crossed the street, Ryan fell in beside Becka. Although he wasn't officially her boyfriend, he was definitely a boy and he was definitely a friend—maybe her best. She liked everything about Ryan Riordan. But it wasn't just his thick, black hair, his sparkling blue eyes, or that heartbreaker smile of his. It was the fact that he was always there for her. And if she needed proof, all she had to do was look at the scar on his forehead—a memento from their last encounter with the Society.

The group had just crossed the street and was standing on the walk in front of the house when Julie came to a stop. "Listen . . . do you hear that?"

Everyone grew quiet. It was faint, but there was no missing the low, quiet whistling—like wind blowing through a screen window, but deeper. It almost sounded like moaning.

"Guys . . ." Krissi sounded uneasy. "I don't think this is such a—"

"Shhh!" Philip scowled.

Julie took a step or two closer. "It's coming from over there." She pointed at the massive brick chimney that ran the height of the house.

"Maybe it's just the wind," Krissi offered feebly. "You know, blowing down the chimney or something."

Becka looked at the oak trees towering over their heads. There wasn't a single leaf stirring. She glanced back at the house—and then she saw it. In the second-story window. "Look!"

But by the time they'd turned, it was gone.

"What was it?" Ryan asked.

"A person. At least, I think it was. I only saw her for a second."

"Probably just the housekeeper," Julie said, not sounding all that convinced.

"I don't think so. It looked like—like a child. A little girl with long black hair."

The group exchanged nervous glances. Becka frowned. "Why? What's that mean?"

"Guys . . ." It was Krissi again. She was leaning on Philip, slightly stooped. "I don't feel so good."

"What's going on?" Becka repeated. She looked at Ryan, but he gave no answer.

Krissi was clutching her stomach now, breathing deeply. Julie crossed to her. "You going to be OK? Kris, are you—"

Krissi shook her head and suddenly convulsed, once, twice—until she dropped her head and vomited.

Becka stood, staring.

Krissi caught her breath, then retched again.

"Come on," Ryan said when Krissi had finally finished. "Let's get out of here."

Krissi looked up and nodded in gratitude as Julie handed her a tissue to wipe her mouth. With Philip on one side and Julie on the other, they helped Krissi back to the car. Ryan turned and followed.

"Ryan . . ." Becka tugged at his arm as they walked. "There's a little girl up there—I'm sure of it. Don't we want to see if she needs help?" They arrived at the car, and Julie and Philip helped Krissi into the back.

"Ryan?" Becka repeated. "What's wrong? What's going on?"

He opened the passenger door for her, then finally answered. He was clearly unnerved. "You know the person that was murdered there? The one who's supposed to be haunting the place?"

"Yeah?"

"It's a little girl."

2

2:04 P.M.

"Just tell me how you can be so sure," Ryan said as the surf washed up and swirled around their bare feet. The water was chilly, but it was still a great afternoon for walking on the beach . . . especially for Becka . . . especially with Ryan. Muttly ran ahead, barking and attacking the foam bubbles with all of his puppy fury.

Ryan continued. "People have been saying that house is haunted for years, and now you come along and say it's just a hoax?"

Becka shook her head. "That's not what I'm saying. I believe there's something there. Absolutely. I just don't think it's the ghost of some little girl."

"But you saw her," Ryan insisted. "You above all people should believe—"

"I saw something, yes. Maybe it was only a reflection. I don't know, maybe it was just the housekeeper."

Ryan snorted. "Come on, Beck. That was no housekeeper."

Becka knew he was right. She also knew it was time to shoot straight with him. But how to begin? She watched Muttly. The foam he'd been chasing was suddenly being sucked out to sea. Unfortunately, that didn't stop the little guy from pursuing it. He ran after the foam, barking for all he was worth, until he looked up and saw a giant wall of water towering above him. He tried to turn, but it was too late. The water crashed down on him, twirling and tumbling him like a stuffed toy, until it finally threw him back up on the beach. He coughed and snorted, looking around all confused.

Becka tried not to laugh. "Ohhh, poor Muttly. . . ." She slapped her leg. "Come here, boy, come on." The dog leaped to his feet and bounded toward her as if nothing had happened. She knelt down and patted him a few times until he spotted another clump of foam and raced off for another attack.

Becka rose and took a deep breath. "Ryan . . . you've been reading the Bible we gave you, right?"

He nodded. "Pretty good stuff."

"Have you run across the part that says if we're away from the body then we're at home with the Lord?"

Ryan frowned. "Meaning?"

"Meaning that once we die, we go straight to be with the Lord. No stopovers at haunted houses. No guest appearances at séances or with Ouija boards. Just death. Then God and judgment."

"So what you're saying is . . . ?"

"That could not have been a little girl's spirit."

"Beck—" there was the slightest trace of impatience in his voice—"how can you deny what you saw with your own eyes?"

"I can only go by what the Bible says."

Ryan picked up a stone to skip. It was obvious he didn't want this to become their first argument. "Look, the Bible makes a lot of sense—especially what it says about Jesus and stuff. But . . . I mean, it doesn't have to be a hundred percent right about everything."

"Why not?"

"Why not?" Ryan paused, trying to put his thoughts into words. "Well . . . it was a long time ago."

"But if we can't believe what it says about everything, how can we believe what it says about anything?"

He opened his mouth to answer, but nothing came.

Becka reached for his hand, making it clear that she wasn't trying to preach. A while back he had started to read the New Testament. Every once in a while they talked about God and Jesus, but it was never a forced thing. Usually Ryan would just have a question, and Becka would do her best to come up with an answer.

But now . . . now they were entering an area in which she definitely had more experience. You don't grow up in the remote Amazon jungles around natives practicing voodoo and witchcraft without learning something about the darker side of the supernatural. Then of course there were the more recent attacks from the Society. Both she and Scotty had learned a lot. Becka took a deep breath and tried again. "Ryan . . . I believe what I saw in the window was not a person."

Ryan nodded. "Agreed."

"But it was not some departed spirit, either."

"Then what?"

"My best guess? It was a demon."

Ryan threw her a look.

She shrugged. "That's exactly what we ran into when Scott was fighting the Society's Ouija board. He thought it was our dad talking to him, but it was nothing more than some demon pretending to be him. My dad's in heaven with God."

Ryan looked out over the water. He didn't agree, but he didn't disagree, either. "And . . . what exactly do you mean by 'demon'?"

"Angels that got thrown out of heaven when they followed Satan."

Ryan looked at her like she had to be joking.

She wasn't.

They walked in silence a long moment, neither sure what the other was thinking. Finally Ryan spoke. "But . . . if you saw a little girl in the window, and it was the same little girl others have been seeing for years, and if a little girl was murdered in that house . . ."

"But how do we know?" Becka asked. Ryan

looked at her and she continued. "Isn't it just like what you were saying about the Bible? If it happened so long ago, how do we know anybody was even murdered there?"

"That's completely different."

"Why?"

"Why?" Ryan repeated. "Well, because . . . because it is, that's why."

Becka grinned. She had him and he knew it. He frowned, then slowed to a stop. "There is one way, though . . . one way to find out."

She searched his face. "How's that?"

"Come on." He turned and pulled her toward the car as he called over his shoulder, "Let's go, Muttly! Come on, fella." The dog gave a couple of yaps, then raced after them.

"Ryan, where are we going? . . . Ryan?"

He gave her a smile. "It's time you and I do a little ghost hunting."

~

2:30 P.M. Darryl, Scott's dweeb friend, approached Cornelius's perch and began teasing the parrot with his finger. Cornelius bobbed up and down, giving an occasional *CRUAWK* or *SQUAWK* of irritation. Darryl paid little attention. "So you really want to get even with the Society?" his voice squeaked. Darryl's voice always squeaked. Today it sounded like part squealing tires and part fingernails on a blackboard.

"Absolutely," Scott said as he plopped on his bed and began cracking sunflower seeds between his teeth. "I'm tired of being their punching bag. I don't know what the Ascension Lady is up to with her séance stuff, but it's time for a little 'eye for an eye.'"

Darryl gave a loud sniff and continued teasing Cornelius. "How're you going to do it?"

Scott cracked another sunflower seed. "Uh, Darryl, I wouldn't be doing that to Cornelius if I were you. He packs a pretty mean bite."

Darryl shrugged and repeated the question. "How're you going to get even?"

"I've been giving it a lot of thought. The surest revenge is to go for the leader."

"You mean Brooke?"

Scott shook his head. "She's pretty much out of the picture since the kidnapping. I'm talking the Ascension Lady."

Darryl's eyes widened in surprise. "Priscilla Bantini?"

Scott nodded.

Darryl gave a nervous sniff. "I don't know. She's pretty heavy-duty."

"So much the better." Scott cracked another seed.

"But . . . I mean, she knows stuff."

"You're saying she's psychic?"

"For starters, yeah. How can you pull off something on someone who knows everything?"

"I'm not sure." He reached for another handful of seeds. "The trick is to find a weakness."

"Good luck." Darryl pushed up his glasses. "Between her psychic abilities, her magic potions, and her astrology charts, she's got everything pretty well covered."

"Astrology charts?" Scott stopped cracking the seeds. "She's an astrology nut?"

"The biggest. She claims it's her 'insight to the future.'"

"So what does she use? Books and charts and stuff?"

Darryl turned back to Cornelius and resumed teasing the bird. "It's all done on computer."

"On computer, huh?" Scott's mind started turning.

"What are you thinking?"

"Your cousin, the computer hack . . ."

"Hubert?"

"You think he might want to help us out again?"

"Depends." He looked back to Scott. "What's up?"

Scott rose to his feet and crossed over to his own computer at the desk. "I'm not sure. Let me check with Z first, see what he knows about astrology."

"You're going to talk to Z? Now?" There was no missing the interest in Darryl's voice. Z was a mystery. The man (or woman—they really didn't know) had become Scott's private source of information on the occult. Z knew everything. And not just about the occult. Sometimes he knew about their own personal lives, things only family would know—which often gave Scott and Becka the willies. But Z would never reveal his identity. They'd even tried to track him down once, but with little success.

Z was always one step ahead.

Darryl pushed up his glasses and gave another obnoxious sniff. "Doesn't he, like, you know, just talk to you at night?"

Scott snapped on the computer. "Usually . . . but I can still leave a message."

Darryl nodded, then suddenly let out a bloodcurdling scream as he grabbed his finger. "OWWWW!"

"*SQUAWK.* MAKE MY DAY, PUNK, MAKE MY DAY!"

Scott looked up from the computer and chuckled. "I told you not to tease my bird."

Darryl glared at Cornelius as the bird continued bobbing up and down, a particularly satisfied gleam in his beady black eyes.

"MAKE MY DAY, MAKE MY DAY, MAKE MY DAY."

~

3:23 P.M. When Ryan had suggested ghost hunting, the last place in the world Becka thought they'd wind up was in the public library. But here they were, inside the dimly lit microfilm-viewing room. Before them were a dozen boxes of microfilm envelopes, with one packet of envelopes for each year that the *Crescent Bay Gazette* had been in publication.

"Here's the last of them," the librarian said with a grin as he hauled in the final two boxes and placed them atop the others. "All one hundred and forty three years. If there's anything about your little girl or her murder, it'll be right here."

Becka and Ryan stared blankly at the boxes. "But where?" Ryan asked. "Where do we start?"

"Well, son," the old man chuckled, "that's your job now, isn't it?" With that he turned and shuffled out of the room. He stuck his head back in to say, "We close at six," then gave them a wink and shut the door behind him.

At first Becka and Ryan were over-whelmed. But soon they started to make headway. Well, sort of . . .

Becka remembered the Ascension Lady wanting the séance the day after tomorrow; that was Friday, the twenty-first. "She'd said the twenty-first was some sort of window," Becka explained. "The anniversary of the girl's murder."

Ryan nodded. "Then that's the date to check."

Becka moaned. "But that's one hundred and forty-three issues."

Ryan flashed her his famous grin. "Guess we'd better get started, then."

Reluctantly she reached down and turned on the bulky microfilm machine in front of her. The screen glowed and a little fan inside began to whir. Ryan followed suit with his own machine.

"Let's start with last year and work back-ward," Becka suggested.

The hours dragged on as they went through year after year. Some of the history was interesting, but for the most part it was a continual stream of boring who-did-what-to-whom or who-built-this-and-bought-that.

Because of the date, there were frequent articles on the Easter season and various church services. This got Becka to thinking about their previous conversation. "Hey, Ryan, how come you believe all this stuff happened—" she nodded at the pile of microfilm—"but you don't believe the Bible?"

Ryan threw her a glance. "Run that past me again."

"Why do you accept all this stuff as history, but not the Bible?"

"Well, this stuff was accurately reported. It was witnessed by the people who lived here."

"And the Bible?"

"It's thousands of years old."

"And?"

"Well, there's nobody around to prove it."

Becka thought this over as she continued going through the microfilm. Ryan had a point. And yet, no one was alive today who could prove George Washington was the first president. Or that Columbus had sailed to America. Before she could put these thoughts into words, Ryan let out a groan.

"What's wrong?" She looked over to his machine. He was on the last microfilm. "There's nothing here; we missed it." He leaned back in his chair and rubbed his eyes. "We've gone through every April twenty-first issue, and there's nothing, not a thing."

Rebecca closed her eyes. She hadn't realized how tired she was.

"So," Ryan continued, "for all these years that murder has only been a rumor? No one was really killed at the mansion?" He looked at her and raised an eyebrow. "That means your theory about no ghosts might be correct."

Becka nodded, grateful that she'd been proven right. But the victory was short-lived. Soon Ryan was tapping his finger on his jaw, the way he always did when he thought. "Unless . . ." She watched. He continued, "If the murder took place on the twenty-first . . . Oh, man . . ."

"What?" Becka asked. "What's wrong?"

"It wouldn't be in the papers on April twenty-first. That's the night it happened. If it was a murder, it would be in the paper the next day or the day after that."

It was Becka's turn to groan. Her eyes were tired and her neck was stiff. But he was right. "Does that mean we have to start all over again?"

"Not if you don't want to." She caught the twinkle in his eye. "If you want to concede and admit you were wrong, that's OK with me."

"No way, bucko." She grinned. "If you can hang on, I can hang on."

"What a man." He smirked. "What a man."

She gave him a look, and they started all

over again from the top—this time checking out April twenty-second and twenty-third.

In less than an hour, Becka found it. The article was dated April 23, 1939, and the headline read, "Man Arrested for Murder of Maid's Daughter."

"Take a look," she said. Ryan joined her, and they read the article together:

Mr. Daniel Hawthorne was arrested Friday evening and charged with the murder of his housekeeper's daughter, Juanita Garcia, age eight. Juanita's mother, Mrs. Maria Garcia, had been employed by Hawthorne for nine months. Both mother and daughter were citizens of Mexico. Friday evening, around 10:00 P.M., neighbors heard what was described as the screaming of a little girl and telephoned the police. Juanita was found on the second-story bedroom floor, lying in a pool of blood. She had been stabbed countless times. Police Chief Warren believes the girl underwent extreme suffering before her demise. Hawthorne has denied all charges despite the fact that when police arrested him, his face and neck were scratched, his clothing was torn, and he was covered in blood. Hawthorne offered no explanation for his condition.

The more Becka read, the lower her heart sank. Not only over the little girl's fate, but also because of her own defeat. And maybe the Bible's. Granted, just because a girl was murdered in that house didn't automatically mean the place was haunted by her ghost. But there was something else gnawing at Becka.

Ryan noticed her expression. "Beck, you OK?"

She continued staring at the screen. "That girl, Juanita, she was from Mexico?"

Ryan nodded. "Lots of rich families had Mexican servants. Why?"

"The little girl I saw up in the window . . . she had dark hair and skin. She could have easily been Mexican."

3

11:54 P.M.

Once again Scott had a difficult time getting to sleep. His mind churned with anger—and with thoughts of revenge. He ran scene after scene through his head, thinking of ways to get even, to make the Ascension Lady look like a fool.

He rolled over and looked at his radio

clock. It was hard to make out the exact time through his dirty socks, but he knew it was late. A thought came to mind. He threw off the covers and padded across to his computer. He snapped it on, typed in a few command strokes, and called up the computer bulletin board. He moved and clicked the mouse only to discover that Z had left a message.

To: New Kid
From: Z
Topic: Astrology

Good to hear from you. Most occult experts think astrology is foolishness. Even your Bible mocks those who believe it: "You have advisors by the ton—your astrologers and stargazers, who try to tell you what the future holds. But they are as useless as dried grass burning in the fire. They cannot even deliver themselves! You'll get no help from them at all." (Isaiah 47:13-14)

FACTS:

*Astrology is the belief that lives are controlled by the position of the stars. The theory has several holes. First, it was conceived and based on the idea that the stars rotated around the earth. (Most of us have discovered that's not true.) Second, there are different versions of astrology with many directly opposing each other. Some believe there are 8 signs of the zodiac; others believe 12, 14, or even 24. Third, it is difficult to find any two astrologers who will give the same advice to the same person on the same day.

Even with these holes and a lack of any supporting scientific evidence, people still believe.

* God is opposed to practicing astrology for many reasons:
1. It takes away our freedom of choice. After all, "It was in the stars—what could I do?"
2. It's turning to sources other than God for your hope, future, and well-being.
3. It's a form of manipulation. Since we're all open to suggestions if somebody or something tells us we will be doing a certain thing, we may just find ourselves starting to do it.

As far as supernatural powers, astrology is like any other superstition: It has no power unless people allow it to direct their lives. For this reason, although it is one of the silliest forms of the occult, it can still harm those who insist upon believing it.

Z

Scott read the final line again: "It can still harm those who insist upon believing it." A smile slowly crept across his lips. "It can still harm those who insist upon believing it." He reached over and shut off the machine.

Somewhere in the back of his head that still, small voice was whispering, *It's wrong. Stop seeking revenge.* But as he crossed back to bed and crawled under the covers, he was able to push that voice aside and replace it with another:

It can harm those who insist upon believing it.

ᔑ

12:10 A.M. THURSDAY Rebecca's mind reeled with the new information on the little girl. Maybe Ryan was right; maybe the Bible couldn't always be trusted. Maybe with the big picture, yes. But after all those years, maybe some of the details had been tweaked or changed.

She slept restlessly, tossing and turning, dreaming of pretty little Mexican girls with long black hair and pleading eyes. Then she heard knocking. Reluctantly she pried opened her eyes.

Knock-knock-knock-knock.

For the second night in a row, Becka threw off her covers, staggered into the hall, and stumbled down the steps. By the time she reached the door, the knocking had stopped. She snapped on the porch light and checked through the peephole. Nobody.

She unlocked the door and stepped outside. The air was cold and the fog was thick, but nobody was in sight. With a sigh she stepped back in. Then, just before closing the door, she noticed a small black case on the doormat. Frowning, she bent down and picked up a videocassette. An envelope was taped to the top.

Becka took one last look up and down the street, then closed the door. As usual she had to give it an extra push before it would shut. She fumbled to snap on the light in the entry hall, then squinted under the glaring brightness. She opened the envelope and pulled out a letter.

Dear Rebecca,
The alignment is less than 48 hours away. I understand your fears and doubts. But please, please remember the child desperately needs our help. This video documents research by a group of parapsychologists who investigated the house back in 1993. Please look it over and get back to me. We have so little time remaining.

Priscilla.

Becka stared at the letter, feeling a chill— along with her growing doubts.

10:15 A.M. Scott and Darryl crossed town, entered a dilapidated two-story house that hadn't seen paint since Columbus took up sailing, waded up a stairway covered in thousands of electronic gizmos and gadgets (not to mention empty pizza boxes), and finally entered the room where Darryl's cousin, Hubert, worked his computer magic. To say Hubert was an eccentric hermit might be rude. To say that the guy ate, drank, slept, and breathed computers (while never bothering to shower) would at least be accurate.

Scott and Darryl had used Hubert's computer genius once before to track down Z. Of course, they'd failed, but that wasn't Hubert's fault. Hubert was good. Very good. Z was just better. A lot better.

"So . . ." Hubert wiped his nose with the back of his hand. He didn't bother looking up. He was too busy soldering something from the mountain of electro-junk before him. "You want this Priscilla person to pull up a bunch of bogus zodiac info on her computer in hopes that she'll follow it, right?" He gave a loud sniff and pushed up his glasses, which looked identical to Darryl's except for the masking tape holding them together.

"Yeah." Darryl gave a sniff back to him. "Can you do it?"

As if to answer Darryl's sniff, Hubert gave another sniff (it was easy to tell these two were related). "No sweat. I build you a Remote Data Acquisition Device, you break into her place, hardwire it directly to her CPU's data bus, make sure she calls up all necessary data onto her monitor, then you break back into her place, remove the R-DAD, and return it to me."

Scott and Darryl traded uneasy looks.

Darryl cleared his throat and asked hopefully, "And then you'll be able to make her do what we want, right?"

"No way." Hubert took another swipe at his nose. "Next I'll need to rewrite her existing program, give it to you, you'll have to break back in the place for a third time, load it into her computer, and exit without being detected."

Scott's heart sank. "Isn't there, you know, any easier way?"

"Easier?" Hubert scoffed. "You want easier!?"

"Well, yeah. . . ."

"You didn't say you wanted it easy." Hubert sighed his best why-am-I-surrounded-by-morons sigh. Then, still without looking up, he produced a single computer disk. He handed it to Scott and said, "Just stick this into her computer."

Scott and Darryl stood dumbfounded. "That's it?"

"Of course that's it." Hubert gave a louder-than-normal sniff. "It will provide me access to her main data bus and mass storage through her modem, where I can ascertain the specific astrological program and download it to my system. Most likely it will be a program from which I can surreptitiously procure the source code, which is no doubt written in language C+, thereby allowing me to reconfigure her program to produce any response you desire."

"Oh," Darryl said, exchanging blank looks with Scott.

"Of course." Scott nodded.

There was a long pause. Darryl and Hubert both gave loud sniffs.

"So," Scott asked, "how soon can we do this?"

"Load her computer tonight, then come back here while I work on the program. By tomorrow morning, she'll do whatever we say." Hubert gave one loud and extremely long sniff, making it clear that their meeting was over.

Moments later Scott and Darryl were scampering down Hubert's rickety porch steps toward their bikes.

"That cousin of yours sure has a brain," Scott said.

"Yeah," Darryl said, drawing in a deep breath of fresh air and obviously enjoying it. "Too bad we can't convince him to try a shower."

Scott grinned as he climbed on his bike. "Once he changes Priscilla's chart, you're sure she'll follow it?"

"Hey," Darryl sniffed, "if it's on her astrological chart, she'll do it. I've listened to her talk about this stuff. Believe me, she'll do whatever it says."

Scott began to smile. He liked that idea. A lot.

They rode off. "So when do you want to do it?" Darryl asked.

"Do what?"

"Load this disk," Darryl said, patting the shirt pocket that held the disk.

"How 'bout tonight? Can you get us in?"

"A piece of cake. What time?"

"I don't know. How does midnight sound?"

"Perfect." Darryl grinned. "The Bookshop tonight, at midnight."

~

5:48 P.M. Julie paused her VCR, and the group stared at the freeze-frame picture on the screen. Becka had taken the videocassette over to Julie's house, and after viewing

41

it, they had decided to invite Ryan, Krissi, and Philip over for a "second opinion."

"There," Julie said, pointing to the screen, which showed a long hallway full of doors. Several cameras and measuring devices were scattered up and down the hall. "This is where it gets interesting."

Julie pushed the Pause button, and the video started again. Everyone watched in silence. For several seconds nothing happened. Then, ever so gradually, some of the papers and charts on the hallway floor began to stir.

"Did someone open a window?" Ryan asked.

No one answered. The wind grew more intense. Some of the instruments mounted in the hallway began to shudder. Suddenly one with aluminum cloth stretched between brackets blew over and fell with a crash.

Krissi gave a start.

"Hang on," Julie said. "It's not over yet. Keep your eye on the farthest door, the one at the end of the hall."

More seconds passed. The wind increased until suddenly the door flew open. The entire group jumped. As they watched, a small shadowy figure from inside the room darted past the doorway and out of sight.

"What was that?" Ryan demanded.

Julie pressed Slow Motion Rewind. The

figure reappeared, moving backward. When it was in the center of the door's opening, she pressed Pause.

"Wow," Philip said as he dropped to his knees and got a better look.

"What is it?" Krissi chirped a little nervously.

"That's what we want to know," Julie said. "It's so far away and so blurry, it's hard to tell."

Everyone continued staring. "It looks like a little girl," Philip finally said. He moved closer to the screen and pointed. "See, here's her hair, long and dark, it's blowing all over the place, and this, this could be an arm. . . ."

An eerie silence stole over the group.

Finally Ryan turned to Rebecca. "Is this who you saw in the window yesterday?"

Becka looked at the ground.

Ryan continued—not mean, just perplexed. "And you still don't think it's a ghost?"

When Becka answered, her voice was just above a mumble. "I'm . . . I'm not sure. It looks just like the girl, but Scotty and I—" she glanced up and held Ryan's gaze— "we've been fooled before."

"I think we should all go there and investigate," Philip said.

Becka answered quietly. "I don't think that's such a good idea."

"Why not?" he insisted. "You might be in danger if you go with the Ascension Lady. I say we go ahead of time and check out the place."

Becka swallowed, struggling to find the right words.

Ryan reached out and touched her shoulder. They'd had enough talks about the supernatural for Ryan to know what was on her mind. "Beck's afraid because we're not Christians. She's afraid we might get hurt."

A strange sort of silence filled the room. Finally Julie spoke. "Is that true? Is that what you think?"

Becka searched for the words. She didn't want to sound high-and-mighty or judgmental to her friends, yet they deserved to hear the truth. "The Bible says there's no such things as ghosts. Only demons."

"And angels," Krissi interrupted, trying to sound cheery. "Don't forget angels."

"Angels don't go around haunting houses," Julie corrected.

Becka hesitated, then continued. "So, if I'm right, that little girl is not a ghost, but . . . a demon."

Philip asked the next question. "And you're worried about us, because . . . ?"

Here it comes, Becka thought. *There's no getting around it.* "Because Jesus gave those who

believe in him authority over demons."
There—she'd said it. She took a breath and
waited.

"And the rest of us?" Philip persisted.

"I . . ." Becka looked down. "I'm not sure
of the details."

After a moment, Krissi blurted, "Hey, I'm
a Christian." The group turned to her in
vague surprise. "Sure, I go to church every
Christmas, sometimes Easter, too."

Everyone chuckled. "I think there's more
to it than just that," Ryan said kindly. "From
what I've been reading in the Bible, it's not
just a church thing; it's what you believe
inside . . . and what you do with it."

Becka looked at Ryan. He gave her a wink.

"I say we investigate anyway," Philip
insisted. "Take our chances."

"And if we're wrong?" Julie asked with an
arched eyebrow. "If it's more than just a
ghost?"

"Then we got our own personal Ghostbus-
ter." Philip gave Becka a playful nudge.
"Right, Beck?"

She smiled feebly.

"When?" Julie asked. "I mean if the Ascension Lady wants a séance tomorrow night,
then we should probably do it—"

"Tonight," Philip finished for her. "Let's
grab some eats and hit the place about eight."

"Sounds good to me." Julie grinned.

Ryan also nodded, but more slowly as he kept a careful eye on Becka.

"I don't know, guys," Krissi whined, her hand going to her stomach. "Not after yesterday."

"Come on, babe." Philip grinned encouragingly. "I'll be right beside you. It should be fun."

"Yeah," Julie agreed, "it'll be fun."

Becka's eyes drifted back to the frozen image on the TV screen. Somehow, *fun* wasn't exactly the word she had in mind.

"Beck?" She turned to see Ryan at her side. He spoke quietly. "You going to be all right?"

She nodded.

"How 'bout Scotty?" he asked. "It might not hurt to have him along."

Becka broke into a grateful smile. Of course he was right. It wouldn't hurt to have her little brother along. It wouldn't hurt one bit.

Or so she thought. . . .

4

"Hey, check this out," Scott said as he pulled his Bible closer. "Remember when Jesus cast those demons out of that guy and into the herd of pigs?"

Becka looked up from her Bible and notes, which she had spread out on the kitchen table. "Yeah, so?"

"Do you know why Jesus sent them into the pigs?"

She shrugged.

"Because—" Scott looked down and read: "'They begged him repeatedly not to order them to go into the Abyss.'*"

"The abyss? That's hell, isn't it? The 'bottomless pit'?"

Scott nodded. "And from what this says, it's so bad even the demons don't want to hang out there. Cool, huh?"

Cool wasn't exactly the word Rebecca had in mind. She glanced at her watch. "Look, we've got less than an hour before we go to the mansion. Let's stick to the subject and keep getting ready, all right?"

"This *is* the subject," he said defensively. "Well . . . sort of."

She gave him a look, then turned back to her notes. Ever since their first encounter with the Society, she and Scott had started paying a lot more attention to spiritual warfare— jotting down verses from the Bible, sharing information. Now, before they went to the mansion, they'd agreed to review what they'd learned and to spend some time praying.

"OK," Becka said, then cleared her throat. "First, we know about the armor of God."

"Check," Scott said. "The shield of faith, the sword of the spirit, the helmet of . . . whatever. We've been through all that already."

Becka hesitated. She wasn't too thrilled by Scott's careless attitude, but she continued. "Second, we know Christ gives us authority over Satan."

Scott leaned back, put his hands on top of his head, and quoted: "'I have given you authority over all the power of the Enemy,' and 'Whatever you bind on earth is bound in heaven.'"

Becka was impressed. She looked back at her notes. "Here's one on Satan: 'There is not an iota of truth in him. When he lies, it is perfectly normal; for he is the father of liars.'"

"Meaning?"

"Meaning we shouldn't believe what Satan or his little demon creeps say."

Scott nodded.

"Here's another: 'If two of you agree down here on earth concerning anything you ask for, my Father in heaven will do it for you.'"

"OK, all right," Scott said, nodding again. "Let's get down to the agreeing part." He closed his Bible with a thump. "Let's do some praying and get going."

Becka glanced at her notes. There were a dozen more verses . . . but because of time— and Scott's impatience—they would have to wait. Reluctantly she closed her Bible. Something didn't feel right. She couldn't figure out what, exactly, but it made her nervous.

Very nervous.

"Dear Lord . . . ," Scotty started, his eyes closed. Becka bowed her head and joined him.

8:03 P.M. "How're we getting in?" Ryan whispered.

"Don't these old places have coal chutes or something?" Julie asked, shining her flashlight along the back of the house. "You know, some sort of slide thing that goes into the cellar?" The group huddled together in the thick, dripping fog near the back kitchen entrance of the mansion. They were well out of sight of the street.

"We could always break a window," Krissi suggested.

Scott smirked. "Only if we want the neighbors to call the cops."

"So what do we do?" Julie demanded.

"How 'bout using the door?"

They turned to see Philip effortlessly push open the back kitchen door.

"How'd you pull that off?" Julie asked.

Philip held up a single key. "My dad's the realtor, remember?"

The others snapped on their flashlights

and stepped through the door into the darkness. Julie led the way, followed by Krissi,
Philip, and Ryan. Rebecca and Scott were
the last to enter. Scott was scowling hard and
rubbing the back of his neck.

"You OK?" Becka asked.

He nodded. "I've got the world's biggest
headache."

"From what?"

"I don't know. It came on real sudden,
soon as we crossed the street."

"You want to go back, stay in the car?"

"Forget it." He tried to smile and make
one of his jokes. "I'm in the mood for kicking a few demons' behinds, aren't you?"

It was Becka's turn to force a smile. Scotty
wasn't just bragging—though he was pretty
good at that—he was also speaking from
experience. He'd faced demons several
times before and come out the winner.

Each time, she and Scotty had fought, and
each time, thanks to prayer and God's
power, they had won. Barely. But barely was
close enough.

But tonight . . . tonight something was
wrong. She was growing more and more
sure of that. Besides the uneasy feeling she
couldn't seem to shake, there was also the
fact that Scotty was feeling sick. Scotty hardly
ever got sick. And, as far as she knew, he

never had headaches. So what was going on?
For the time being she said nothing more.
But she would keep a careful eye on him.

Once inside, things went pretty much as
expected. After the initial goofing off—grabbing and scaring each other—they settled
down to exploring the ground floor.

First there was the kitchen. It was massive:
double ovens, pantry, lots of counter space,
cupboards. *Mom would go nuts here,* Becka
thought.

Next came the dining room, then the
music room, then the glass-enclosed conser-
vatory, and finally the giant entry hall.

"Wow," Philip exclaimed as they shone
their lights on the rich mahogany paneling,
the towering gilded mirrors, and a floor that
was completely covered by thick gray slate.

Everyone was impressed. Everyone but
Scott. He was standing off to the side,
hunched over and holding his head.

"Hey, Scotty," Ryan asked, "what's wrong?"

Scott lowered his hands and tried to smile,
but it was more of a grimace. "I don't know.
My head . . . it's like a herd of elephants tap-
dancing inside."

Becka and Ryan exchanged looks.

Krissi was shivering. "I'm cold. Couldn't
someone turn up the heat?"

"Uh, I don't think so," Philip chuckled.

"Look at this." Julie was slightly ahead of the group, shining her light up at a giant crystal chandelier. It was directly over her head and breathtakingly beautiful. But it wasn't the beauty she was referring to. It was the movement of the crystals. They had started to gently clink against each other.

"Must be wind," Ryan offered, but he didn't sound too convinced. He turned back to Scott and Becka. "You were the last ones in. Did you guys shut the door?"

"Yeah," Becka answered softly, "we shut it."

The clinking grew louder as the chandelier started to sway almost imperceptibly.

"Well, now." Julie tried to sound glib. "I think maybe we should be moving on. Don't you?"

The group voiced agreement and continued forward, keeping a wary eye on the chandelier and going out of their way to avoid walking directly under it.

They arrived at the stairway. It was massive, sweeping up and above their heads. They stood a moment, looking in awe. Finally, Julie asked the inevitable. "OK, troops . . . who's going first?"

Everyone exchanged glances, but no one answered. Philip looked over his shoulder and smiled mischievously. "Becka? Scott? This is your guys' department, right?" There were a couple of nervous snickers. Philip kept looking at them, waiting for an answer. "Well?"

Scott finally stepped forward, doing one of his hokey superhero imitations. "You're right, earthling. Step aside. This is no job for mere mortals." The group chuckled as Philip happily obliged.

Becka was a little more reluctant, but she also moved forward to join her brother. She hated it when he played Mr. Macho—especially when it involved her life (or death). "What about your head?" she whispered.

"Hey—" he forced another smile—"we're the good guys, remember?"

"Scotty—"

"Come on." He motioned for her. "Let's show your friends some ol'-fashioned ghostbustin'."

"Scotty . . ."

Without a word, he started for the stairs. Becka stared after him a moment, then gave a heavy sigh and followed.

The banister was made of dark wood with intricately carved designs. Elaborate stained-glass windows towered to the right, along with rich curtains trimmed in gold braid. The group had only traveled three or four steps before they noticed the breeze. It was faint at first but seemed to increase with every step they took.

To relieve the tension, someone began whistling the theme from *The Twilight Zone.* "Knock it off," Julie ordered. They did.

"Philip . . ." Krissi was somewhere in the back whining again. "Philip, I'm cold."

But instead of answering her, Philip said, "Listen! Do you hear that?"

It was a low whistling, the same one they'd heard from the chimney the day before. As the wind grew stronger, the sound grew louder. Becka threw a nervous glance at Scotty. He was squinting and grimacing, trying his best to hold back what appeared to be intolerable pain. Beads of sweat were forming on his forehead. "Scotty," she whispered, "Scotty, are you OK?"

"We've beaten these things before," he answered. "If we've got the faith, there's no reason we can't beat them now."

Becka had no answer. He was right—but something was wrong. Terribly wrong.

They were halfway up the stairway. The breeze increased. The whistling grew louder, its low drone sounding more and more human.

"I'm so cold." Krissi shivered. "Isn't anybody cold?"

"It's just your nerves," Julie said.

Philip shook his head. "I don't think so."

"Me, neither," Ryan said. "Check it out."

He held the flashlight up to his mouth and blew. They could all see his breath.

"Let's go back!" Krissi shuddered. "We've seen enough."

"We're practically there," Philip insisted. "Let's go on."

Becka and Scott resumed the climb. The wind blew harder, tugging at their clothes and hair. Becka looked back to her brother. He was also shivering. Violently. But it wasn't from the cold; she knew that. It was from something else. Maybe the pain. She leaned over to him. "Scotty, we don't have to go any further if—"

"Be quiet," he hissed through gritted teeth.

She pulled back a little surprised. "What?"

"The Bible says we've got authority, so we've got authority. If you don't have the faith, fine. But don't pull me down with you."

Becka could only stare. This wasn't like him. Not at all.

The eerie droning grew louder, sounding more and more like a muffled cry—as if someone was trying to scream but was being smothered.

At last they reached the landing, Becka and Scott first, followed by the others. They stood silently on top. To their right was a dust-covered window; to the left was the hallway.

All eyes moved down the hall to the last door, the one they had seen on the videotape.

The cry broke into a shriek—a blood-curdling, heart-stopping shriek. Long and continuous.

"Let's get out of here!" someone shouted.

They turned to race back down the stairs when, suddenly, the door at the end of the hall flew open, crashing loudly into the wall. The group froze. But it wasn't the wind that had thrown open the door. It was a shadow. A dark shadowy creature, looking very much like the little girl. It exploded out of the room and flew down the hall at them.

Krissi screamed. Others joined in as they scrambled for the stairs. Everyone but Scott. Instead of running, Scotty spun around to confront the shadow. From past experiences, he knew what to do. He raised his hand and, despite the throbbing in his head, he shouted, "In the name of Jesus Christ of Nazareth, I command you to—"

He said no more. The shadow smashed into him, directly into the center of his chest. He gasped and reeled backward until he hit the wall beside the window and slowly slid to the floor.

"Scotty!" Becka raced to him.

Others stood staring, dumbfounded.

"Scotty!" Becka dropped to his side. "Scotty, are you all right?" The shadow girl was gone, but the wind was still shrieking, and she had to shout to be heard. "Scotty!"

His eyes fluttered, then opened. He looked dazed and confused. "What . . . what happened?"

That's what Becka wanted to know. She brushed the hair out of his eyes, searching his face for clues. She reached for his arm to help him up. "Come on, let's get you out of—"

He looked down at his chest, and suddenly his eyes widened in horror. "Get them off!" he shouted. He started slapping and hitting his chest. "Get them off!"

"What?"

"Get them off!"

"Get what off?"

"The flies!" He began to writhe and kick, all the time beating and slapping at his chest. "Get them off! Get them off!"

Becka was at a loss. "Scotty, there are no—"

"Get them off!" He was screaming. "Get them off!"

"Scotty!"

"Get them off! There's millions of them!"

She reached for his hands, trying to stop him, but he knocked her aside, continuing to slap and hit and shout and writhe.

Ryan joined their side. "It's OK, Scotty."

"Get them off!" Scott was starting to cry, tears streaming down his face.

"It's OK. We'll get them—just come with me." Ryan slipped his arm under Scott's shoulder and raised him to his feet.

"Get them off! Get them off!"

"It's OK. We're going to get you out of here."

Becka rose to follow Ryan, but as she turned she felt something cold and damp brush against her skin. She spun around to the window beside where Scott had hit the wall. In the dust a design had started to form . . . all by itself. Becka felt herself growing colder.

But she would not turn away. As she watched, she began to realize it wasn't a design that was forming. It was letters. Words. Someone or something was writing on the dust of the windowpane. The letters formed slowly, but they did not stop until the message was finished. It read:

¡Ayúdame! ¡por favor, Rebecca ayúdame!

Becka's Spanish was rusty, but not that rusty. She knew what it said: *Help me! Please, Rebecca, help me!*

~

10:58 P.M. The group had barely entered the car before Scott tried to cover his fear with a *Ghostbusters* joke. "I think I've been slimed," he said, gingerly testing his bruised ribs. But the humor fell flat. Maybe it was because his voice still had a slight tremble. Or maybe it was because of the tension that filled each member of the group.

Without a word, Ryan fired up the Mustang, and they started for home.

"I don't get it." Krissi finally broke the silence. "You kept shouting about flies."

"That's 'cause there were thousands of them, they were all over me—I was crawling with them."

"And yet we didn't see a thing," Julie said. "How weird."

"When did they leave?" Philip asked. "When did they all disappear?"

Scott looked down at his arms and chest just to make sure they had. "I don't know," he answered more quietly. "I guess—I guess by the time we got outside . . . definitely by the time we got off the property."

More silence as all of the kids fell into their own thoughts . . . and fears.

Rebecca's mind reeled. First, because of Scotty's defeat. Weren't they supposed to have authority through Christ over this sort

of stuff? And second, because of the writing
on the window.

It had been in Spanish. Juanita's language.

Becka looked around the car, wondering
if she should tell the others. No, that type of
information would only support their theory
that this was not some sort of demon, but
that it was actually the little girl's ghost.

As they pulled up to the front of Becka
and Scott's house, Ryan finally spoke. His
voice was earnest. "I don't think you should
be a part of that séance tomorrow, Beck."
Rebecca looked at him. He took a deep
breath and slowly let it out. "But if you
decide to go . . . then we should all go along
with you."

More silence. Slowly each member of the
group started to nod. Philip cleared his
throat and said what each was thinking.

"Ryan's right. That ghost thing definitely
has it in for you two. And if we're there with
you . . ." He hesitated.

"There's safety in numbers," Ryan finished.

"Oh, really," Scott quipped, still massaging
his chest. "I hadn't noticed."

Becka looked at them. They were friends.
Good friends. And she appreciated them
now more than ever. "Thanks, guys." She
tried to smile. "I'll let you know."

She opened the car door. After they said good night and the car pulled away, Scott and Becka headed for the front porch. Becka opened the screen door. It gave its customary groan. And then she saw it—the front door was not completely shut. The thing always stuck, and if you didn't give it an extra pull, it always stayed ajar.

"Scotty . . ." Her voice grew thin and wavery as she pointed to the door.

Scott saw it, too.

"I'm sure I closed it," Becka said in a half-whisper. "I always give it an extra yank."

Scott swallowed. "Me too."

They traded looks. Steeling himself with determination, Scott reached for the knob. He turned it and gave a push. It squeaked as it unstuck.

There was no other sound.

Scott entered the darkened living room, slowly, cautiously. Becka was right behind. He headed toward the nearest lamp. It was eight feet away, but it could have been eight miles. Why hadn't they left a light on before they'd gone? Then again, that had always been Mom's department. Across the room, over by the kitchen, Becka noticed the tiny red light blinking on the telephone answering machine. There were two messages.

She watched the outline of Scott's body

bumping into furniture and stumbling over clothes and stuff they'd left in the middle of the room (another disadvantage of not having Mom around). He made progress toward the lamp, but far too slowly.

Then, from the hallway, Becka heard a faint snarl. At first she thought it was her imagination. She strained, listening harder. There it was again.

"Scott . . ."

Before he could answer, there was sudden, animallike clawing. Whatever it was, it had decided to make its move. It raced down the hallway, digging into the carpet, heading directly for them.

"Get that light!" Becka screamed. She could see nothing in the dark, but heard the thing tear into the room and bear down toward her. She hunched over, bracing for impact.

Suddenly the room was flooded with light as Scott clicked on the lamp to reveal—

"Muttly!" they cried in unison.

The animal leaped at Becka's legs and began bouncing and jumping all over her feet. It had been hours since he'd had any company, and the puppy was all squirming body and wagging tail. Becka stooped down and patted him. "Hello, boy, good dog, easy now, easy . . ."

Scott had already started for the kitchen. "Check it out," he said, pointing to the table. "It's a note." He snapped on the kitchen light, and Becka moved in for a better look. It was a note with a key on it.

Dear Becka and Scott: Just swung by to see how everything's going. Here's the key your mom left. Hope you can make it to youth group tomorrow. Call if you need anything. Love, Susan

There was a notable sigh from both brother and sister. Susan was the youth worker from church. She must have dropped off the key, then left without knowing she had to yank the door shut.

"I guess you might say we're a little wound up," Scott said wearily.

Becka agreed.

Scott crossed to the fridge (as he always did when he got home), and Becka headed for the answering machine (as she always did when she got home). She pressed Play.

"Hi, guys, it's Mom. Beck, I had the weirdest dream about you last night. Kinda spooky. I'll have to tell you when I get back. Aunt Bernice's funeral is tomorrow. I should make it home by noon, Saturday. Don't forget the leftover casserole in the fridge, and Beck, please, *please* make sure Scotty's wearing clean T-shirts. Love you guys. Bye. *BEEP.*"

Scott gave a sniff under his arms. "It's good for a few more days," he called. He stuck his head back into the fridge and resumed his search-and-devour mission.

The second message began.

"Hello . . . this is Priscilla Bantini—from the Bookshop."

Becka froze.

"Juanita, or her spirit, told me what happened tonight. She wants me to say how sorry she is. You snuck up on her and frightened her, that's all. Please call me at your earliest convenience. *BEEP.*"

"Frightened *her!*" Scott exclaimed. "*We* frightened *her??*"

"I don't get it," Becka sighed as she shed her jacket. It was time to say what had been rattling in her head the past twenty-four hours. "Maybe Ryan is right; maybe we can't trust the Bible in every instance."

"Whoa, hold the phone," Scott said as he pulled his head out of the fridge. "What are you talking about?"

Becka flung her jacket across the room to the growing pile of clothes on the sofa. "Figure it out. We're Christians, right?"

"Right."

"We're supposed to have authority over demons, right?"

"Right."

"Well, no offense, little brother, but you weren't exactly the conquering hero this evening."

Scott said nothing as he closed the refrigerator and crossed to the table. In his hands were a carton of milk, a jar of dill pickles, and some dijon mustard. Not exactly a gourmet meal, but it was the best he could come up with on such short notice. He pulled a pickle from the jar and dipped it into the mustard. Becka watched, trying not to retch as he crammed half of it into his mouth. She could tell he was as troubled as she was; he just expressed it differently . . . by becoming a human garbage disposal.

She turned and headed for the stairs. But just before she arrived, she heard a very quiet and very heartfelt "I'm sorry, Beck."

She slowed to a stop and looked at him.

He continued softly, slowly, "I let you down. . . . I let us both down. I'm sorry."

Becka's heart went out to him. "It's not your fault." She shrugged. "Things just aren't making sense anymore." He continued to look down, and she went on, "The Bible says there are no ghosts, yet we run into ghosts. It says to put on God's armor, to use his shield and sword to beat demons. We do and we get clobbered."

"But we've won before," Scott said, looking up at her.

Becka nodded. "Not this time. This time . . . everything's going haywire." She paused a moment as they both thought through the evening. "Listen," she finally said, "you don't mind if I use the computer to call up Z, do you?"

"I don't know that you'll get him," Scott answered as he wolfed down the second half of his mustard-covered pickle. "I doubt he'll be on-line, but you're welcome to try."

Becka nodded and started up the stairs. Everything was unraveling: her confidence, her little brother's strength, her faith in the Bible. Then, of course, there was tomorrow night . . . the infamous séance. Should she go? Was tonight a warning that they should prepare harder?

Or was it an omen of an even darker encounter, a showdown that would lead to even greater defeat?

5

11:33 P.M.

 It had taken
Becka twenty minutes to log on to the computer bulletin board. It would have taken
two minutes, but Rebecca's computer skills
were as bad as Scott's eating habits. After
five or six attempts, she finally got on-line.
And to her surprise, Z was there waiting.

> Good evening, Rebecca. This is our first time
> alone, isn't it?

Rebecca swallowed back her nervousness and typed:

> Hi.
> How was your evening?

She caught her breath. Did Z know about their visit to the house? Or was he just fishing? She thought about asking, then decided to skirt the issue and move on.

> I know this isn't your area of expertise, but is there a way, I mean, what real proof do we have that the Bible is 100% true 100% of the time?

There was a pause. A moment later the following verse appeared:

> "The whole Bible was given to us by inspiration from God . . ." 2 Timothy 3:16.
> You mean people got all worked up and inspired by God so they started writing a bunch of—
> No. In the original language *inspired* means "God-breathed." So all Scripture is breathed by God.

Becka thought a moment, then typed:

> But just because the Bible says it's true . . . Just because something says it's true, doesn't mean it's true.

There is other evidence. Jesus believed the Bible was accurate. He quoted from it frequently. In fact, when he fought Satan in the wilderness, that was all he used. Think about it—a battle between the most evil force in the universe and the Savior of the universe. They could choose any weapons they wanted, but instead of swords or guns or nuclear bombs, they used what both knew to be the most powerful force in the universe . . . God's Holy Word.

Becka nodded. He had a good point. She typed back:

Everybody says it was written so long ago. . . .
That is correct. But in all of history there is no other book that has been proven to be so completely reliable. Again and again historians and archaeologists uncover other historical writings and ancient artifacts that prove the Bible's accuracy.

Becka stared at the screen. She was relieved. Yet, how could the Bible be so accurate when everything she had experienced in the past twenty-four hours seemed to prove it was so wrong? She looked up as the final set of words appeared:

It is late. I must sign off, but you must promise

me one thing.
What's that?
Whatever your decision may be regarding
tomorrow night, promise me you will be very
careful. There is far more danger than meets the
eye.
Z

Becka's mouth dropped open. Quickly
she reached for the keyboard and typed:

Z? How do you know these things, Z?

But there was no answer. Only the last set
of words:

Be very careful. There is far more danger than
meets the eye.

~

12:11 A.M. FRIDAY Scott hadn't bothered to
tell Rebecca about the little breaking-and-
entering routine he and Darryl had cooked
up for that night. He figured she had
enough on her mind. Come to think of it, so
did he. But a promise was a promise. And
revenge was sweet no matter what time of
day . . . or night.

"Give me a boost," Darryl's screechy voice
whispered.

Scott laced his fingers together and held
open his palms. Darryl stepped into them,
and Scott hoisted him up to the tiny bathroom window at the back of the Ascension
Bookshop.

Darryl had gone into the bookstore a few
hours earlier, when it was still open, snuck
into the bathroom, and unlocked the window. "I saw this on an old *MacGyver* epi-
sode," he squeaked, "or was it *Matlock*?
Come to think of it, maybe it wasn't either.
Maybe it was—"

"Just push open the window and get
inside," Scott whispered.

"I can't reach it. Let me stand on your
shoulders."

Before Scott could protest, Darryl scrambled out of Scott's hands, up his chest, and
onto his shoulders—leaving plenty of greasy
tread marks along the way.

"Oh, man," Scott whined as he looked
down at his T-shirt.

"I still can't reach it. Let me stand on your
head."

"Do what?!"

"I'm too short to reach the window. Let
me stand on your head." Again Darryl's little
feet scrambled, and again Scott wound up
with tread marks—this time across both ears
and his forehead.

Suddenly a voice demanded, "Whad—whad're you doin' down here?"

The boys froze. Because of Darryl's weight on his head, Scott couldn't turn, but he shifted his eyes as far to the right as they would go. It was Mr. Leery, the town drunk, staggering home after another long night of tipping brews. Mr. Leery continued his stumbling approach until he was staring directly up at Darryl, who was towering a good five feet above him.

"S'not right, you boyz bein' here."

Scott's mind raced. Mr. Leery was right, of course. Standing in a back alley, breaking into a bookstore at midnight was not exactly the role of a model citizen. So what was this old man going to do? Blow the whistle on them? Call the police? And what was Mom going to think when she came home and had to bail her son out of jail?

"Great," Scott moaned silently, "just great."

Mr. Leery wagged his head from side to side. "S'not at all right. You—you shudn't be here," he repeated as he continued staring up at the giant before him. "The Lakerz are playin' tonight—you should be with the res' of yer team, gettin' thoze rebounds and makin' them fanzy bazkets . . . they need you, boy."

Mr. Leery threw a look up to Darryl. The

little guy nodded down at the man but said nothing.

Mr. Leery nodded back, pleased that he'd made his point. "Go—go get sooted up then," he ordered and held out his hand, waiting for a high five.

Darryl reached out and obliged. Of course Mr. Leery didn't quite connect with his hand, but it was close enough. The old-timer turned and staggered away, pleased that he'd done his part to help the L.A. Lakers toward another championship.

Scott stared after him. He knew his mouth was hanging open, but he didn't much care.

As soon as the man staggered out of sight, Darryl burst out laughing.

"Come on," Scott ordered, "you're killing my head."

Darryl resumed twisting and turning atop Scott's skull (grinding in any grease he hadn't already wiped off on Scott's face and T-shirt) until he finally pushed open the bathroom window and squirmed inside.

"How long will it take?" Scott whispered up to the window.

"Just long enough to get her computer up and load in the program. Ten minutes max."

Scott breathed a sigh and threw another cautious glance up the alley. He looked down at his stained T-shirt and began rubbing the top of his head. This revenge business sure could be painful. He glanced at his watch. They still had to run over to Hubert's and get him to reprogram the astrological charts. But with any luck, they'd have the Ascension Lady making a major fool of herself by morning.

12:54 A.M.

Earthquake!

The thought exploded in Becka's mind and sent her bolting upright in bed. Having moved to California, she figured she'd eventually experience some rocking and rolling from Mother Nature. She just hadn't planned on experiencing it quite this soon. But here it was.

Or was it?

Her room was lit by only an outside streetlamp that shone through the window, but even then she could tell that nothing else in the room was moving. Not her bookshelves, not the lamp on her nightstand, not even the water in the fishbowl on her dresser. Only her bed.

She laid her hand on the mattress. It wasn't her imagination—the bed really was vibrating. Not a lot, but enough.

Next she noticed the cold. Saw it, really.

White puffs of breath coming from her mouth . . . exactly as they had in the mansion. She threw a look to the window. It was closed. Even if it had been open, it was spring outside. And spring in this part of the country did not mean this type of cold.

The shaking increased. Soon the headboard started banging against the wall. But there was another sound, too. A buzzing—faint at first, then it grew louder and louder with the shaking. Becka pulled the blankets up around her. Part of her wanted to leap out of the bed and run for her life. And part of her was too frightened to move. For the moment, the "too frightened" part was winning.

She shivered. But it wasn't from the cold or even from the fear. It was something else. She couldn't put her finger on it, but there was something even icier, even more frightening, in the room. Something she'd felt before. . . .

Her heart pounded. It was the same cold dampness that had brushed against her in the hallway of the mansion. And now it was touching her face.

The shaking of the bed turned to violent lungings. The buzzing sounded like a thousand flies circling her head, like a chain saw roaring. She opened her mouth to yell to

BILL MYERS

her brother in the next room, but no sound
came. The cold dampness had wrapped
itself around her throat and was quickly
tightening its grip. She tried breathing, but
her air was being shut off. It was strangling
her, suffocating her.

It was trying to kill her.

She reached to her neck, clawing at it, trying to peel whatever it was away. But there
was nothing to grab. Just icy dampness. Her
lungs pleaded for air. She twisted and strug-
gled, trying to draw in the slightest breath.
No air would come.

The bed was bouncing out of control, its
headboard crashing into the wall with every
leap. Becka's lungs burned, screaming for
air. The outside edges of her vision started
to grow white. She was going to pass out; she
knew the signs. She had to do something,
and it had to be fast. Mustering all of her
strength into one final act of defiance, she
lunged forward and—

Becka bolted awake in bed.

It had been a dream! She sat on her bed,
gasping for breath, filling her lungs with pre-
cious oxygen and her mind with blessed reality. Strange. Everything had seemed so true, so
real. It was definitely not your average night-
mare. But she was awake now. She was safe.

Yet, even as she sat there, catching her

breath, forcing herself to relax, she noticed something that sent another chill through her body. Small white puffs of breath were coming from her mouth. The same chill she had felt in her dream was there, in her room. The same cold dampness. And this time it was for real. She looked at her window and sucked in her breath. A thick layer of frost had formed . . . on the inside.

"Scott!" she called. "Scotty!" There was no response.

She threw off the covers. She was getting out of there. She was not falling victim to this thing a second time.

Her feet barely touched the floor before she stopped. The skin on her arm prickled as something icy touched it. The sensation traveled up her arm and across her body, making her give an involuntary shudder. Then it was gone. Almost. Whatever it was, it was still in the room.

She'd had enough. This was her bedroom—she wasn't about to be driven out of her own room. She cleared her throat and demanded, "What . . . who are you?" There was no answer, but she would not be put off that easily. "I said, who are you?" Still no answer.

Then, remembering all that she and Scotty had learned about spiritual warfare,

Becka tried again. "In the name of Jesus Christ, I order you to reveal yourself."

Becka watched and waited in speechless anticipation. Soon the air began to ripple. In the middle of the room an image wavered and slowly formed. At first it appeared to be a darker version of the darkness that already filled the room. A shadow within a shadow. But gradually it took shape. Features slowly formed. Becka gasped. Although it was still transparent, there was no mistaking who it was. Little Juanita.

Becka tried to swallow, but her mouth was as dry as cotton. "What . . . what do you want?" she demanded.

The girl turned to her, cocking her head as if she didn't quite understand.

"What do you want?"

The image shimmered and grew more solid. Now it was possible to clearly see the girl's face. She was puzzled, confused, and very, very frightened. Remembering the writing on the window, Becka tried again, this time in Spanish, "¿Quién es? ¿Qué quieres?"

Before the girl could answer, another image suddenly rippled in the air and formed to her left. It seemed to be a handsome woman with long, beautiful hair. She wore an expensive black nightgown. Becka had only seen her once but recognized her immediately. It was Priscilla, the Ascension Lady.

Priscilla looked to Becka with her tired, sad eyes and smiled. Then, turning her attention toward the girl, she knelt down and reached out her arms. It was an offer of help, of comfort. At first the girl resisted, afraid to come near. But the Ascension Lady waited patiently, making it clear that she was there to help.

At last Juanita took a tentative step toward her. The Ascension Lady smiled broadly. Encouraged, the girl stepped closer. Then closer again. The Ascension Lady continued to smile, waiting.

Another step, and then another. Now the little girl was standing directly in front of the woman. Becka watched as, with great tenderness, the Ascension Lady reached out and wrapped her arms around the helpless child.

There was no missing the gentle affection. The woman looked over to Becka and smiled.

But the smile suddenly froze. Her expression turned from joy to surprise . . . and then to horror. There was a tearing sound, as if something was ripped. The woman screamed, her voice shrill and agonizing as she grabbed her stomach and fell back from the girl.

The little girl turned to Becka, confused, afraid, and looking very helpless. But in her hands were shredded pieces of the woman's nightgown.

The Ascension Lady was writhing on the floor, screaming, holding her stomach in agony. Juanita looked down at her with deep pity . . . and confusion. Then, without warning, she leaped on the woman and began beating her with powerful blows and clawing at her with suddenly razor-sharp fingernails. The woman screamed and tried to protect herself, but she was no match for the child's superhuman strength and animallike claws.

Somehow, for a brief second, the Ascension Lady managed to pull herself free from the girl. That's when her eyes found Becka's. They were full of anguished pleading. "Help me," she gasped, reaching for Becka. "Help—" Before she could finish, the girl leaped on her again, and again she tore into the woman.

Becka managed to shake herself from her horror. "Stop it!" she screamed. "You're hurting her!"

The girl did not hear.

"I order you to stop!"

Instead, Juanita reached out and, to Becka's astonishment, picked up the woman, lifting her as easily as though she were a stuffed doll. She raised the Ascension Lady effortlessly over her head, then flung her across the room. Priscilla hit the back wall hard and slid to the floor in a daze. The girl looked puzzled over what she had done, as though confused at her own powers.

Becka took a step closer and shouted. "You're hurting her! I command you to stop!"

Juanita paid no attention. She began searching the room, looking for something. Then she found it. The lamp on Becka's nightstand. In a flash she leaped to it. She grabbed it, ripped off its shade, and bounded back to the Ascension Lady.

For a moment she stood over the groaning woman, looking down at her with pity and compassion. Then slowly, sadly, she raised the lamp high over her head.

Becka understood what was coming. Whether the child knew what she was doing or not, she had to be stopped. Becka was certain that if she didn't do something, the girl would smash the lamp into the semiconscious woman. She stepped closer and angrily shouted, "Stop it! I command you to stop it and leave my room!"

The little girl turned to her. This time her confusion was mixed with hurt. But hurt feelings or not, she had to be stopped. "In the name of Jesus Christ of Nazareth . . ." Becka faltered. The little girl had started to cry. Becka watched a moment, unsure what to do. Tears streamed down the sad little face, but Becka forced herself to continue. "In the name of Jesus Christ of Nazareth, I command you to go. Leave!"

The child was sobbing now. Helplessly. Uncontrollably.

Becka bit her lip. What was going on? Was she doing the right thing?

With the lamp still poised over the Ascension Lady, Juanita looked at Becka. Her face was stained with tears; her bottom lip trembled with emotion. Her eyes seemed to plead with Becka, as though she hoped she would give her permission to finish the job.

Becka shook her head. "No. I command you to leave! Leave my room, now!"

Juanita's expression dropped even lower. She turned as if to leave, then suddenly raised the lamp and brought it crashing down on the woman's chest.

"Nooo!" Becka screamed. "I command you to leave! Leave my room! *Now—!*"

Rebecca shot up in bed, wide awake. Another dream! A dream within a dream.

She quickly reached for the lamp on her nightstand. It was time to flood the room with light, with reality.

But the lamp was not there.

She threw off the covers and raced to the wall switch by the door. She snapped it on and squinted as the overhead light glared into the room, replacing the darkness with bright, cleansing light. The brightness hurt her eyes, but it was a small price to pay.

Until the light revealed something across the room, near the corner. It was hard to make it out at first, since it had been broken and the shade ripped off. But after a second, Becka realized she was staring at the shattered lamp from her nightstand.

6

4:32 A.M.

"Hi, Scotty."

Scott gave a start as he entered his bedroom and fumbled to turn on the light. He saw Becka sitting at his desk in the dark. "What are you doing here?" he asked in surprise.

"My room was getting a little crowded for sleeping."

"What?"

"Never mind. Where have you been? It's 4:30 in the morning."

Scott was exhausted. It had been quite a night . . . and morning. First there was that little field trip through the Hawthorne Mansion, then the visit to the Bookshop. And finally, for the past few hours he'd been working with Hubert as they dreamed up false info for the Ascension Lady's astrology charts.

"Where have I been?" he echoed. "Let's just say your friend at the bookstore will have a brand-new look the next time you see her."

"My friend . . . the Ascension Lady? You've done something to the Ascension Lady?"

"Not me." He smirked. "She'll be doing it to herself. It's all in the stars . . . and her computer." He pulled off his jacket and tossed it on the growing pile of clothes in the corner.

"What did you do?" she asked.

He waved her off. "It's a long story, but the lady will definitely be sporting a new 'do the next time you see her." He gave a long, noisy yawn. "Right now I'm bushed." He started peeling off his T-shirt.

Becka had been sitting there almost an hour trying to think what she should say when he came back. Should she tell him more about her growing doubts? What about the experience in her room? What about her decision to visit the Ascension Lady to try and warn her?

It looked as though she had just wasted her time. Scotty, with his usual male egocentrism, wasn't interested in anything but his own accomplishments . . . and, of course, sleep. She got up and started for the door.

He gave another yawn. "What were you saying about your room?"

"Forget it," she answered. She would say nothing more. At least for now. If he was lucky, maybe she'd leave a note on the table, letting him know she'd be at the Bookshop. But as far as anything else, it looked like she'd have to work things out on her own.

"Hey, Beck?"

She stopped in the doorway and turned.

"So what's the deal? Are you going to that séance tomorrow?"

She took a deep breath and slowly let it out. "I don't know, Scotty."

~

2:10 P.M. Becka stood outside the Ascension Bookshop. The sign on the door read Closed for Lunch. She peered through the posters and stickers plastered over the window and saw someone rummaging around inside.

"I hope I'm doing the right thing," she sighed as she reached out and rapped on the door. She waited, folding her arms against the cold . . . not the cold of the morning, or even the cold of fear. But the cold of gnawing uncertainty.

She ran through it all again. Was the little girl a demon or Juanita's ghost? The Bible said there are no ghosts. OK, fine. If that was true, then why was the girl Becka had seen the same age as Juanita? Why did she look like Juanita would have looked? Why did she speak Spanish like Juanita surely must have done?

Then there was the question about a Christian's "spiritual authority" . . . all that stuff in the Bible about beating the devil. Why wasn't it working for Scotty? Why wasn't it working for her?

Finally, there was the love question. Granted, Juanita wasn't exactly the most likable being, but even in her dream Becka was pretty sure the kid was acting more out of fear and confusion than meanness. And the Ascension Lady was the only one trying to help. Not Becka, not Scott. Only the Ascension Lady was reaching out in love.

That's how Becka saw it, anyway. And that's why she was there. She had to warn the Ascension Lady. No matter how much the woman wanted to help Juanita, who knew what would happen to her if she went through with tonight's séance?

Becka heard the bolt unlock. Then the door to the Bookshop swung open. But it was not the Ascension Lady who greeted her. Or was it?

Instead of the long black hair, this woman had a closely shaved buzz. And it was tinted red. But that was nothing compared to her breath. A wave of garlic stung Becka's nose, making her eyes instantly water.

The woman broke into a smile. It was the Ascension Lady's smile. And those were her eyes—those same sad, frightened eyes. "Rebecca, please come in." She opened the door wider, and Becka stepped inside.

The Bookshop was not at all what she had expected. Instead of dark, foreboding shelves covered in spiderwebs, and a handful of witches standing around stirring cauldrons, this place was bright and cheery. Sunshine poured through overhead skylights. The floor was covered in aqua blue carpeting, the shelves were white and inviting, and the books they held looked friendly and colorful.

"Sorry about my breath," the Ascension Lady laughed as she shut the door. "It's all part of my new identity."

"Identity?" Becka said, trying to blink back the tears.

The woman nodded. "After our rendezvous last night, I realized I had better change my identity."

"Rendezvous?"

"Yes, our little get-together in your room."

Becka's heart skipped a beat. "You were there? You saw what happened?"

"Of course I was there. Didn't you see me?"

Becka was stunned. "But I thought . . . I mean . . ."

"You thought it was a dream?"

Becka nodded.

The Ascension Lady smiled. "I was astral projecting—leaving my body while I slept. It's not an uncommon practice, not for those of us involved in the deeper secrets of New Age. In a sense, I suppose you could say I was dreaming too. But not really."

"So . . . you saw what happened?"

"Oh yes—" the Ascension Lady smiled and rubbed her abdomen—"and felt it."

Becka could only stare.

The woman crossed toward the counter. "It was all symbolic, of course. But it made clear to me the drastic actions that had to be taken for tonight."

"Was cutting your hair part of that drastic action?"

The woman ran her fingers over her shaved head. There was a trace of sadness to her voice. "It really wasn't my decision." She picked up a clove of garlic on the counter and popped it into her mouth, between her gum and teeth. She winced as it burned, yet she continued to suck and chew. "But it all made sense after this morning's forecast."

"Forecast?"

"My astrological forecast. Great things are going to happen to me tonight, but I must keep my identity hidden. In fact, the charts have never been more specific—they even said I should shave my hair, and dye it—I shaved my eyebrows, too; did you notice?

As Becka stared, a faint bell sounded in her head. Scotty had said something about the Ascension Lady sporting "a new 'do."

"And, of course, these garlic cloves—" the woman fanned her mouth, indicating how much they burned—"they are to help me alter my normal olfactory signature."

"Your what?"

"My scent. That way I won't be recognized by my scent either."

Becka continued to stare, wondering if the woman had any idea how foolish she looked, or sounded . . . or smelled.

"In all my years I've never encountered an astrological forecast like this one. But when

I read it on the computer this morning, I knew something was happening."

Becka closed her eyes. Computer, astrological forecast, shaved head. She knew what was "happening." Or who. Scotty. This woman's absurd looks and crazy actions were all Scotty's doing.

Rebecca cleared her throat and tried to change the subject. "So you're, uh, you're still going tonight, even after all that happened in my room?"

"Juanita's just confused," the Ascension Lady explained. "She just misunderstood my actions. But with a new identity we'll be able to start over, and I'll be able to reach her." The woman turned and looked directly into Becka's eyes. There was no missing her sincerity. "She needs us, Rebecca. You know that now. You have seen it yourself."

Becka glanced away.

The Ascension Lady approached. Her voice was full of understanding and compassion. "I know you're frightened. I know you're starting to have doubts about your beliefs."

Becka bit her lip. It was as if the woman had read her mind.

The Ascension Lady reached out and gently touched Rebecca's arm. Becka's eyes met the older woman's gaze.

"It's alright to feel as you do. Supernatural experiences often help expand our too-limited views of God."

Becka tensed. What was she saying? That her doubts were right? That the Bible couldn't be trusted? That God wasn't who he said he was? No! This was wrong! And yet . . .

"Please," the woman continued, "I know it is unnerving, but search the Christ within you, and see if he would not have you reach out to this little girl in his love."

Becka continued to look into the woman's eyes.

"Join with me. We are not enemies. We are coworkers. We are on the same side. The side of love."

The woman was making more and more sense. "But what . . ." Becka cleared her throat, trying to find her voice. "But what about Juanita's powers? Aren't you afraid of them?"

The Ascension Lady laughed gently. "Of course I am. I am terrified. That is why I need you at my side. We both saw how you were able to help me last night. She may attack again, only more violently."

"And you'll go, even if I don't?"

"I must. She needs me. She needs us."

"Becka?" A voice spoke from the door.

Becka turned to see Ryan. He looked puzzled and concerned.

"Ryan," she exclaimed, "how'd you know I was here?"

"I called your brother. He read your note." Ryan continued checking out the situation and the woman. "Listen, we need to talk. There's something at the library you need to see."

For a moment Becka was torn. For a moment she actually didn't want to leave the Ascension Lady.

"Now," he said firmly.

"Oh . . . yeah, sure." She started toward the door.

"Rebecca?"

Becka turned.

"I will be starting at eight. Your friends are also invited."

Becka looked at her and nodded.

~

3:34 P.M. "I still don't get why you were there," Ryan said as he slipped a microfilm into the machine and snapped on the switch. The light came on and the fan whirred quietly. "You're the one who said she was evil."

"I . . . I might have been wrong," Becka answered. "She's only trying to help. When you think about it, aren't we really both fighting on the same side? For the little girl?"

Ryan looked up at her from the machine. His expression made it clear that he had his doubts. Come to think of it, so did she.

Without a word he directed his attention back to the screen and started to adjust the microfilm as he said, "The more I've been thinking about what you said about the Bible, the more this whole thing's been bugging me."

Becka looked on, waiting.

"I mean, you're right. Either the Bible's true or it isn't. So I got here early this morning and started going through the newspapers again." At last he had the microfilm lined up. "Take a look at this."

Becka leaned over and read the headline: "Hawthorne Hill: Site of Holy Rituals."

She glanced to Ryan, who nodded for her to continue reading. It was a 1988 interview with an older Native American from the area. He spoke of having hunted and fished in various locations that were now parts of the city. A few paragraphs later he spoke of Hawthorne Hill, the location of the mansion:

It had always been a sacred place. Our grandfathers, our great-grandfathers, and their fathers before them practiced their magic on that hill. It was a place of strong power. Spirits frequently

appeared. Even as children we knew
this was no place to play.

Becka came to a stop. She did not have to
read further.

Ryan spoke quietly. "There were things
happening on that hill long before Juanita
was ever murdered there. Probably centuries
before."

Becka nodded.

Ryan continued, "So what we saw in that
house . . ."

Becka finished the phrase for him:
". . . may not have been the girl's ghost, but
one of those evil spirits."

Ryan looked at her a long moment and
then slowly nodded.

7

5:45 P.M.

*B*ecka looked
out the car window at the passing houses. "I
just wish there was somebody I could run all
this stuff past. With Mom gone and Scotty
playing Rambo, there's nobody."

"What about Z?" Ryan asked as he eased
the Mustang around another corner.

Becka glanced at her watch. "Z usually

doesn't come on-line till nine. The séance will already be going."

Ryan gave a heavy sigh. "I still don't think you should go."

Becka glanced at him. Her heart fluttered, moved by his constant concern for her. Who else would spend all Friday morning in the library trying to prove her right and himself wrong . . . just to make sure she would be safe? Ryan was a treasure. One she hoped never to lose.

She looked back out the window. "If I don't go, will that stop Julie and the others from showing up?"

"No way, they're making it a major event."

"And it sure won't stop the Ascension Lady. If I don't show, who knows what will happen to her."

"But she's your enemy."

Becka looked back to him. "She's trying to do right; she's just all mixed up. Besides, even if she was my enemy—"

"I know, I know," Ryan interrupted. "'Love your enemies.'" He threw her a mischievous grin. "I've been doing my reading."

Becka laughed. "But do you believe it?" Her comment carried a double meaning. She wasn't just asking if he believed in a Bible verse. For several weeks he'd been flirting with making a commitment to Christ, and for several weeks he'd been reading the Bible, trying to decide.

He looked over to her and quietly answered. "I'm almost there, Beck. Just give me a little more time."

Becka nodded. She wouldn't rush him. Even if she could stand for a little more Christian company . . . especially tonight.

"I've got it!" Ryan suddenly said. "Susan, from the church. The one who helped rescue you from those satanist guys."

Relief flooded Becka. "Of course! Why didn't I think of it? Mom even asked her to check in on us."

Without a word Ryan threw the car into a U-turn and they were off.

~

7:07 P.M. "But if this thing is a demon, shouldn't Beck and her brother have been able to, you know, make it obey them? I mean, isn't that what the Bible says?" Ryan was pacing back and forth in Susan's tiny office. He seemed more agitated than Becka.

Susan leaned forward on her desk, listening. As usual she was working late. She was a college student and a newlywed. She and her husband, Todd, worked part-time as youth pastors for the Community Christian Church.

She had listened with interest to Becka and Ryan's story. When Becka expressed her confusion over the ghost seeming to be real, Susan had nodded.

"I can see why you've started to believe in this thing. But don't forget that demons have knowledge of all that has happened. It wouldn't be too hard for them to masquerade as the little girl who was killed there."

"And they could speak Spanish?" Ryan had asked.

"They could speak whatever they wanted," Susan had agreed. "If Spanish is called for, that's what they will use."

Now Susan nodded again at Ryan's insight. "Yes," she agreed, "in theory, as believers, Becka and Scott should have authority over the demons."

"So what gives?" Ryan's voice had an edge of impatience. "Becka has a special guest appearance in her bedroom, Scotty's attacked by flies, and—"

"Wait a minute . . . did you say flies?"

"Yeah, thousands of them. Why?"

"One of his names . . . one of the names God gave Satan was Beelzebub."

"Be-elle-za-what?" Becka asked.

"Beelzebub. It's like one of God's jokes on him. It means 'Lord of Flies.'"

Becka felt the old familiar chill run across

her shoulders. It took a moment to find her voice. "So what you're saying is we might be dealing with more than just a demon?"

Ryan stopped pacing and looked at the women. "You're not talking about—I mean, are you saying it might be *Satan?*"

Susan shrugged. "Hard telling. Lots of times demons will claim that very thing to try and freak you out. But from what you've described, with the history of occult activities on that hill, whatever they are doing is definitely big-time."

"They?" Becka repeated. "You said *they.*"

"You're probably dealing with a cluster of them, yes."

"But why do they always appear as Juanita's ghost?"

"Ghosts, angels of light, spirit guides— demons come in all sorts of disguises."

"Still, the Bible says we have authority over them, and my brother tried and got trounced. Why?"

"A good question." Susan reached over to her shelf and pulled out a Bible. She began leafing through the pages. "Christians shouldn't go out looking for fights with the devil. After all, his job is to kill and destroy. But when they meet him, they will win if they are using God's power."

She found her place. "Ah, here we go,

Ephesians 6:12: 'For we are not fighting against people made of flesh and blood, but against persons without bodies—the evil rulers of the unseen world, those mighty satanic beings and great evil princes of darkness who rule this world; and against huge numbers of wicked spirits in the spirit world.'"

Becka nodded. "I know. Believe me, Scotty and I are very familiar with those verses."

Susan continued. "There's more: 'So use every piece of God's armor to resist the enemy whenever he attacks, and when it is all over, you will still be standing up.'"

Again Becka nodded. "But Scotty wasn't exactly standing up. When Juanita—or whatever it was—got through with him, he was lying flat on his back, thinking he was covered with flies."

Susan nodded, still looking at the pages. "Hmmm, there are some conditions. The armor of God is not just some flowery phrase. There are very specific pieces of protection that we need to put on before going into battle."

"Like what?" Ryan asked.

Susan found her place and continued reading: "'You will need the strong belt of truth and the breastplate of God's approval. Wear shoes that are able to speed you on as you preach the Good News of peace with God. In every battle you will need faith as your shield to stop the fiery arrows aimed at you by Satan. And you will need the helmet of salvation and the sword of the Spirit— which is the Word of God.'"

"Man! That's a lot," Ryan said.

"And prayer," Susan concluded, reading: "'Pray all the time.'"

"OK," Becka said, "let's go down the list just to make sure. We've got our sword." She pointed to Susan's Bible. "I'm learning to believe in the Bible, more so than ever. What's the 'helmet of salvation'?"

"The knowledge of your salvation through Christ. When you know you're secure in him, that stops Satan from playing with your head, from fooling you into thinking you're not saved so you don't think you have power."

"Got that," Becka said. "I know I'm saved."

"And if we aren't?" Ryan asked, clearing his throat and shifting a little uncomfortably.

Susan looked at him. "It's your choice, Ryan, but I wouldn't wait too long with all that's coming down."

Ryan nodded. "I hear you."

"What else is in that armor?" Becka asked.

"The shield of faith."

"Faith, I've got that."

"Shoes to spread the gospel." Susan looked up. "You're ready to tell people about Jesus, aren't you?"

"I can vouch for her on that," Ryan chuckled. Becka grinned back at him.

"That just leaves two things. The belt of truth—you're not lying or deceiving anybody?"

Becka shook her head.

"And finally the breastplate of God's approval."

"Meaning?"

"Meaning you're being as righteous as you can . . . and if you mess up, you're asking Jesus to forgive you."

Ryan chuckled again. "Beck and her brother are the squeakiest-clean kids I know."

"You don't have to be perfect," Susan corrected. "You just have to be certain you're trying to be, and that you ask Jesus to forgive you."

Becka started to nod, then caught herself.

Susan was the first to notice. "What's up, Becka?"

"It's just . . . I mean, playing a practical joke on somebody, that's not like sinning, is it?"

Susan smiled. "I think God has a sense of humor. Just as long as nobody's getting hurt or it isn't done out of anger."

"Uh-oh."

Both heads turned to Becka. She took a

breath. "Scotty, he's been playing this elaborate joke on the Ascension Lady, getting her to shave off her hair and stuff."

Ryan started to laugh. "That was Scotty's doing?"

Becka nodded, then turned to Susan. "Is that a problem?"

"It's pretty funny," Susan agreed, nodding, "but it's pretty mean, too."

"He was looking for a way to get even, to get some kind of revenge for all the stuff she's done to us."

A frown crossed Susan's forehead. "Revenge?"

"Yeah."

"So he hasn't forgiven her."

"No way."

"Is that a problem?" Ryan asked.

"Unforgiveness? Yeah, Ryan, that's a big problem. The Bible says we have to forgive, that seeking revenge is wrong." Susan turned back to Becka. "I don't suppose he's asked God to forgive him?"

Becka shook her head. "I doubt it. I think he's having too much fun."

Susan took off her glasses and rubbed her eyes. "I think we've found it—the missing piece in his armor." She stopped, then quickly looked back to Becka. "He's not going to that séance, is he?"

"He knows everyone else is going to be there . . . and he'll definitely want to see his handiwork on the Ascension Lady."

Susan tried to keep her voice calm and even but didn't quite succeed. "He could get hurt, Becka. If he goes in there unprotected, he could get hurt very badly."

Becka looked at her watch. "It starts in less than an hour. Can I use your phone?"

Susan nodded and handed it to her. Becka dialed and waited. A moment later she sighed in frustration as Scott's recorded message came on: "Hi, I'm not. You are. I will be. So leave a message so when I am, I can . . . I think."

After the beep she spoke quickly into the phone. "Scotty, if you're there, pick up. Scotty. Scotty!" No answer. "Listen," she said, glancing at her watch again. "It's 7:20. Don't go anywhere. Do you hear me? Wait till Ryan and I get there. We're on our way. We've got to talk. Don't go." She hung up.

Susan was on her feet, opening her door for them. "Do you think he's left already?"

"I don't know," Becka said as she and Ryan headed out into the hall. "Thanks, Susan."

Susan followed them a step or two. "Be very, very careful."

Becka gave a half-wave as she pushed

open the outside door and headed into the parking lot.

As the door slammed, Susan leaned against the wall. Then she went back into her office, crossed to her desk, and sat a moment. As a Christian, Becka had no business going to a séance. And yet, she had to go to rescue her brother—maybe even the Ascension Lady. . . .

Susan shook her head, then lowered it into her hands and started to pray.

~

7:33 P.M. Becka yanked the front door to her house shut and let the screen slam as she raced back to Ryan's Mustang. She held a wadded piece of paper in her hand.

"Not there?" Ryan called.

She shook her head. "We've got to get to the mansion."

Ryan nodded and fired up the Mustang. "What's the note say?"

She smoothed it out and read: "'Beck: Julie called. They'll meet you there. I'm grabbing a bite to eat with Darryl. Should be fun.'"

Ryan tromped on the accelerator, and they sped off.

8

7:53 P.M.

BANG!

The Mustang careened to the left. Ryan
hit the brakes and fought the wheel, trying
to keep the car on the road.

"What is it?" Becka cried.

"A tire!" Ryan shouted as he slowed the
car and carefully nursed it toward the side of
the road with the sickening *RUTT-RUTT-
RUTT-RUTT* sound of a flat.

"Do we have a spare?"

"Yeah." The car rolled to a stop, and Ryan opened his door. "It's going to take some time, though."

Becka threw open her own door. "Can I help? What can I do?"

Ryan crossed to the back and opened the trunk. "Give me a hand unloading all this junk."

Becka joined him and groaned. The trunk was full of crushed pop cans, a baseball mitt, various pieces of a tennis racket, a partially deflated soccer ball, dirty sweatshirts, torn jerseys, old high-tops, new high-tops, greasy two-by-fours, wrenches, ratchets, and other car junk—along with anything else Ryan had ever used since birth or planned to use until death.

"I know it's in there somewhere," he said.

She gave him a look. He shrugged. They started unloading.

~

8:04 P.M. "It is after eight," the Ascension Lady said. "It is imperative that we be punctual."

"If we could just wait a couple more minutes," Julie said. "I know Becka wanted to be here." She turned to Scott. "She did say she was coming, right?"

Scott tried to focus on Julie. The pounding in his head had returned—so bad he'd barely heard. "Yeah," he mumbled, "sure."

"You don't look so good," Krissi said, adjusting her hair for the hundredth time. "Are you OK?"

"I'll be fine," Scott answered hoarsely. He had come for two reasons. The first was out of good old-fashioned curiosity. Second, he wanted to have a few laughs over the Ascension Lady's new look. Unfortunately, by the time he had joined the others in the mansion's dining room, his head hurt so badly he couldn't laugh. He couldn't even smile.

The Ascension Lady eyed him carefully. She knew something was up; she just couldn't put her finger on it. She turned back to Julie. "I agree with you. I, too, would like to wait for Rebecca. But Juanita has told me her murder occurred at ten at night. The corridor between our two worlds will be open only at that time. If we are to help, I am afraid we must start now."

There were no chairs or tables in the room, so she motioned toward the floor. "Please." She set her camping lantern on the hard wooden floor, dimmed its light, and eased herself down beside it, cross-legged.

Krissi, Julie, Philip, and Darryl exchanged glances. It had been a surprise to see the woman with a dye job and her newly shaved head and eyebrows. Then of course there was her garlic breath. "Well, at least there's no chance of vampires," Julie had giggled. But now . . . now they were about to participate in something they were completely unsure of. Something Becka had warned them about. And something that Becka wasn't even there to protect them from.

Philip was the first to sit. The others followed his lead, a little more reluctantly. But Scott held back. Something inside was telling him this was wrong, very wrong. And more than that—it was dangerous.

"What's the matter?" Darryl squeaked good-naturedly. "You forget your flyswatter?"

The others chuckled nervously.

"I am sorry—" the Ascension Lady was puzzled over the joke—"I do not understand."

Philip explained. "Last night, when we were here, Scott had a little run-in with flies here."

"Flies?" The woman turned to Scott. "You had an experience with flies in this house?"

Scott shook his head. "It was just my imagination, something I thought I saw. No biggie."

The Ascension Lady looked at him very carefully. It was obvious she knew something

he didn't. And it was obvious that it made
her nervous. "We must be careful," she said,
still looking at him. Then more quietly, she
continued, "If you do not wish to join us,
that is understandable."

"No," Scott said, sensing a challenge, "I'll
join you. Why wouldn't I?" As he sat down in
the circle directly beside the woman, part of
him was already kicking himself for being
such a hotshot. *She gave you an excuse. Why
didn't you take it and get out of here?* But there
was another part, the part that knew he had
fought this sort of stuff before and won. The
part that hoped last night's experience was
just an exception and that the authority he
had would still beat the bad guys.

If only his head would stop pounding.

"Now—" the Ascension Lady held out her
hands—"if you would all join hands with
one another to create an unbroken circle."

They took each other's hands.

"We shall start by emptying our minds.
Think of nothing . . . no worries, no cares
. . . let your minds be free and empty."

"No problem for you there, huh, Krissi?"
Darryl cracked.

The others snickered.

"Quiet now." The Ascension Lady
frowned. "You must let your minds be clear
. . . let the peace of the universe prevail."

They settled down. After a moment, Philip cleared his throat. "I, uh, I don't think I can do this." All eyes turned to him. As the intellectual of the group, he was having a harder time shutting down. "I don't know if I can just think of nothing."

The woman seemed to understand. "You must try," she said. "By emptying your mind, you will make it easier to hear from the beyond. You will make it easier for Juanita to communicate."

8:24 P.M. The Mustang raced up the hill toward the Hawthorne Mansion. It squealed to a stop directly behind Philip's car. Changing the tire had taken longer than Ryan had expected, and both his hands and Becka's were smudged with grease and grit. But at last they were here.

"Look!" Ryan pointed through the windshield up to the second-story window, the same window where Becka had first seen Juanita. There were fleeting, shadowy movements inside—fighting silhouettes—one larger, one smaller. A man and a girl. Ryan threw open his door. "We've got to stop them!"

"Who?"

He leaped out of the car. "Juanita . . . or

whatever . . . and whoever it is trying to kill her."

Becka was out of the car, too. "Ryan, no!" Her voice brought him to a stop. "That's not Juanita; it can't be. You said so yourself."

"But—" he pointed toward the window— "can't you see them?"

She looked back up to the window. He was right—there was obviously something going on up there. And it definitely looked like a big man and a little girl. But they'd been fooled before. "No." She shook her head. "I see what I see. . . ." She hesitated, then continued, "But I know what I know."

Ryan looked at her.

"We've been down this road before, Ryan. There are no ghosts. Only demons counterfeiting as ghosts."

He looked back up at the window. The fighting continued.

"It's not real . . . it can't be." She forced herself to look away, to look directly at him. "If we go in, we have to remember that. We have to go by what we believe. We believe the truth, God's truth. The rest of that stuff—" she motioned toward the window— "that's all lies."

Ryan turned to her. "So we're back down to faith, huh?"

She smiled and reached out her hand. He

looked at it, then slowly took it. It was a pact, an agreement. He would do his best to believe. So would she. They turned to face the house. "Let's do it" was all he said. They started across the lawn toward the front porch.

As they reached the massive stone steps, Ryan threw one final look up to the window. The shadows were gone.

They climbed the steps and crossed to a heavy wooden door. Leaded glass panes ran down both sides of the entrance, revealing a faint glow of light inside.

Becka knocked, but there was no answer. "They've already started," she concluded. She grabbed the handle and gave the door a little push. It groaned quietly and opened.

Immediately they were hit by the smell.

"Whew!" Ryan said, fanning the air.

"It smells like rotten eggs," Becka said as she coughed.

"It's sulfur."

Becka turned to him.

He nodded. "I'd recognize it anywhere. It happens in chemistry class sometimes when things backfire. Yes sir, that's definitely sulfur."

"Wonderful," Becka muttered.

"Why, what's up?"

"In the Bible, sulfur's another name for brimstone."

"Brimstone?" Ryan repeated.

Becka nodded. "As in fire and brimstone."

"You mean like hell?"

"Yeah, like hell."

8:32 P.M. Susan raised her head from her desk. She was exhausted. She had been praying nonstop for Becka and Ryan ever since they left her office. And still she felt something was wrong. She knew she had to keep interceding.

She reached for the phone and started dialing. Todd would be home. She needed help; she needed someone to join her. The battle was not over yet—in many ways it hadn't even begun.

8:34 P.M. Becka and Ryan paused outside the entry hall a moment, each making sure the other was determined to go ahead—each unsure if they really wanted to. Gathering all of her strength, Becka finished opening the door and stepped inside. Ryan followed. It was the same entry hall they had visited the night before. The same gray slate tile, the same towering stairway, and the same crystal chandelier.

"Over there," Ryan whispered. He pointed

to a room a couple of doors down, through a distant archway. They could see the faint glow of a lantern reflecting off beige walls. A voice was quietly murmuring.

They started forward. The voice became clearer, and they recognized it as the Ascension Lady's.

"Empty your minds . . . see if she would use you as a vehicle by which to communicate. Juanita, we are here for you. We understand your need, and we have come to help. . . ."

As Becka and Ryan approached the room, the group came into view. Julie, Philip, Krissi, little Darryl, Scotty, and the Ascension Lady—all sitting in a circle holding hands with their eyes closed. The only light was from the camping lantern.

"I sense a presence," the Ascension Lady said. "Juanita, is that you?"

Scotty was the first to sneak a peek at Becka and Ryan as they arrived at the archway. The others followed suit. Everyone but Krissi. She and the Ascension Lady seemed to be oblivious to the newcomers. They were the only ones really getting into it.

"Is that you?" the Ascension Lady repeated. "Juanita, do you have something to say?"

Becka motioned for Scott to join her. He

hesitated. She motioned again. Finally he pulled Darryl's hand over and replaced it in the Ascension Lady's. "Do not break the circle," the woman warned, her voice sounding farther and farther away. "Do not disturb the flow."

Scott silently rose to his feet and stole behind the woman. "I feel movement," she droned. "There is a definite stirring in the spirit world."

Julie and Philip barely held back their snickers. Krissi, on the other hand, was totally gone. "Me, too," she whispered in excitement. "I feel it, too."

Scott followed Becka out of the room and behind the arch.

"You look terrible," she whispered.

He nodded wearily. "I feel it. But I'm not giving in. Not this time. This time we're going to fight to the end."

"No, Scotty." Becka frowned.

"What?"

"You're not ready. You're not protected."

"What are you talking about?"

"The Ascension Lady . . . what you did to her hair, her breath."

Despite the pain, Scotty managed a grin. "Pretty cool, huh?"

Becka shook her head. "No. That's the problem." He looked at her but didn't understand. "Remember with that Ouija board, when they were supposedly calling up Dad—remember that section we'd read in the Bible about the armor of God? The shield and sword and stuff?"

Scotty nodded, then winced. The pain in his head was getting worse.

"Are you OK?"

He took a breath, trying to fight off the throbbing. "Yeah. . . ."

She kept a careful eye on him and continued. "Remember all the parts of armor we're supposed to wear?"

Again he nodded.

"Well, we talked to Susan, and you're missing a piece. The breastplate of righteousness."

"The what?"

"Your pranks against the Ascension Lady, your unforgiveness toward her . . . God sees those things as unrighteous."

Scott stared at her incredulously. "After all the junk she's pulled, you think a little practical joke is wrong?"

"It's not the joke, Scott. It's you. Inside. We're supposed to forgive—you know that."

The throbbing increased. Scott took another breath, trying to hold the pain at bay. "After all they've done to us, you're telling me we can't . . ."

She nodded. "If you're in it for revenge, if you haven't asked God to forgive you for your wrong attitude, that's exactly what I'm—"

She was suddenly interrupted by a terrified scream. It was Krissi. They rushed around the arch and into the room. Krissi was holding her right hand directly in front of her. It was trembling. "My hand," she cried, "what's happening to my hand?"

"Do not fight it." The Ascension Lady was also staring at it. "Do not fight it, sweetheart, do not fight it."

"What's happening?!"

"Let it have its way." The Ascension Lady dug into her coat pocket.

Krissi continued staring. "What's happening? What's happening?"

The woman pulled a tablet and pencil from her pocket. "Don't fight it," she repeated. "It's Juanita, she's wanting to communicate."

The group watched, wide-eyed, as the woman took Krissi's shaking hand and shoved a pencil into it. Then, placing the pad in Krissi's other hand, she commanded, "Write."

"What?"

"Let her write through you. She's using your hand to communicate with us."

"Please," Krissi was starting to whimper, "I don't want this—"

"Let yourself go. I promise you, you will be safe. Just let your hand go; let her write."

Krissi threw a frightened look at Philip. For a moment he was unsure. Finally he nodded. "It'll be OK, Kriss, we're right here with you. Go ahead and do what she says."

Keeping her eyes glued to Philip for support, Krissi lowered her right hand to the pad. As soon as the pencil made contact, the writing began. It was wild and erratic, but she was definitely writing letters.

Julie moved for a better look. "It's Spanish! She's writing in Spanish."

"But . . ." Krissi stared at her hand in unbelief. "I don't know Spanish!"

"Let her have her way," the Ascension Lady kept coaching. "Just relax and don't fight it."

The letters formed quickly and sloppily until an entire sentence was finished. And then the writing stopped. Just like that. Krissi released the pencil and began rubbing her hand.

"What's it say?" Julie demanded. "Does anyone know Spanish?"

Becka stepped farther into the room. "I do."

The Ascension Lady looked up and saw

her for the first time. "I knew you would come." She smiled.

"What's it say, Becka?" Krissi asked anxiously. "What did I write?" She turned the tablet around so Rebecca could see.

Becka felt that old familiar chill. It read: *"Ustedes son míos."*

"What's that mean?" Krissi asked. "Translate it for us."

Becka fought to keep her voice from shaking. "'You are mine.'"

Everyone grew silent. Everyone but Krissi. "'You are mine'? That's stupid. What's that supposed to mean, 'You are mine'?" The group turned to the Ascension Lady. But even in the dim light it was possible to see that most of the color had drained from her face.

"Are you all right?" Julie asked.

The woman stared straight ahead as though she saw something no one else could see. Suddenly she cried out in alarm.

"Stay away! Stay away!"

"Priscilla? Ms. Bantini?" Julie reached out to touch her, but the woman paid no attention to her. Her eyes were wide with horror.

"No!" she shouted. "Not the children! Get away! Get away!"

She threw up her arms just as the camping lantern exploded, sending shards of glass in all directions, plunging the room into darkness and chaos. Everyone shouted and screamed—but none so loudly as the Ascension Lady. "Stay away! I am here to help! Stay away!"

"Turn on a flashlight," Philip shouted. "Someone turn on your flashlight."

"Mine's dead," Darryl yelled.

"Mine, too," Julie cried.

"No, please! Get away! Get away. . . ."

The floor began to shake. Instantly. Hard and violent.

"It's an earthquake!" Ryan yelled.

But this was no earthquake. It was more like a roller coaster gone berserk. The floor rolled and pitched in every direction. Everyone screamed. Unable to stand, unable to crawl, they were bounced and tossed across the room like rubber balls, smashing into walls, hitting doorframes, screaming against the terror and chaos.

"Nooooo!" The Ascension Lady wailed. Her voice rose above their heads. "Put me down! Put me down!"

9

8:57 P.M.

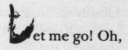et me go! Oh, please, put me down!"

The woman's voice seemed to be rising higher and higher. Something was lifting her above their heads! The floor continued to buck and pitch, and a howling wind filled the room. Just when it seemed the noise had reached its peak, the Ascension Lady was

127

hurled through the arches, toward the entry hall, and up the stairs.

"NOOOOoooo!"

The shaking stopped. So did the wind. There was only silence . . . and the quiet groaning and sobbing of kids.

Then smoke seeped into the room—a freezing, impenetrable fog that filled the darkness. With the smoke came an even stronger smell of sulfur. It was overwhelming, burning the back of Becka's throat, making her eyes water. The voices around her grew louder—coughing, groaning, weeping.

"Help me . . . please. . . ." The cry was weak, but Becka immediately recognized the whine. It was Krissi. She sounded as though she were just a few feet to the right.

"Krissi, Krissi, are you all right?"

"My face . . . what happened . . . to my face?"

Becka rose to her knees and crawled blindly in the fog and darkness toward the voice. "Krissi, what's wrong?" She reached the girl's leg, then felt her way up her body toward her head.

"My face . . . Becka . . ."

"It's OK, Krissi. I'm right here, I'm right here."

At last Becka felt the girl's shoulders. The fog was so thick she had to bring her eyes in very close to see. Krissi had both hands covering her face. Becka pried them away. And then she gasped.

The beauty queen's face was shriveled like a piece of old dried-up fruit. The sagging eyes and drooping mouth belonged on a two-hundred-year-old hag, not a seventeen-year-old beauty.

Krissi saw the horror in Becka's eyes, and her hands instinctively shot back to her face. Carefully her fingers traced the wrinkles. "Becka . . . help me. . . ." Tears spilled down Krissi's cheeks as her fingers explored every crevice, every fold. "What's happening?"

Becka felt a wave of revulsion sweep over her, but Krissi was her friend. She pulled the hideous face into her arms. "It's OK, Krissi. It's OK."

"My face . . ." She was crying now. "Dear God . . . not my face . . . please . . . please, make it stop, Becka. Make it stop."

As Becka held Krissi, her mind raced. What was happening? Was this for real? Or was it another demonic counterfeit? What could she do?

"Beck?"

Her ears perked up. "Scotty," she called. "Scotty, over here."

She could hear him crawling toward her. When he arrived he looked more haggard than ever. "What happened?" he gasped. "What's going on?"

"I don't know. I've never heard of anything like this."

"Are we . . ." He hesitated. "Are we in hell?"

The thought sent Becka reeling. She fought it back instantly.

"No, we can't be. We're Christians. This is demonic. It's an illusion."

Scott grabbed his head and winced. "Aughhh!"

Becka watched helplessly as he battled the pain. It lasted for several seconds. Finally he looked up to her. "That was a beaut."

"Scotty, listen to me. You've got to protect yourself. You've got to get rid of your unforgiveness." He looked at her blankly. She grew more frustrated. "I can't fight this myself! You've got to forgive the Ascension Lady and help me!"

Before he could answer, there was another cry, weak and pathetic. "Help me, help me. . . ."

"It's Philip," Scott said.

"Please . . . help me. . . ."

He spun around and disappeared into the fog.

"Scotty! Wait!"

He didn't. "I'm right here, Philip," Scotty called. "Where are you? What's wrong?"

The voice was full of fear. "I . . . I . . ."

Scott followed the sound. A moment later he found Philip curled up in a little ball, eyes wide in fear. "Philip, what's wrong?"

"I . . . I . . . Scotty, I don't know anything. . . . My mind . . . it's, it's . . . going."

"No, man," Scotty answered. "It's a trick. They can't do this sort of thing."

"But I—I'm stupid! I don't . . ." He paused a moment as if trying to remember something. Suddenly he blurted, "I can't even remember my name. Help me!"

"It's a trick. They're messing with your mind—"

"Please! Help me, help me. . . ."

"Becka!" Scotty called.

"Right here," she answered. She emerged through the fog, half dragging, half carrying Krissi.

As Krissi grew close enough for Philip to see, he gasped, "Who are you?"

Krissi began sobbing uncontrollably.

"Look," Becka ordered, "you two, stay put! Stay right here. Scotty and I, we'll find the others."

"No! Please, don't leave me here," Philip begged. "I wouldn't know . . . I don't know where I am. I don't know how to get out."

"Right now, none of us do," Scotty answered.

"Becka . . . ," another voice wailed. "Becka . . ."

Rebecca recognized it instantly. It was Julie—straight ahead, near the center of the room. She eased Krissi against Philip. "Stay here. I'll be right—"

And Darryl's voice, off to the left. "My eyes, I can't see . . . my eyes . . ."

"I'll get him," Scott said. "You take care of Julie."

Becka nodded and made her way through the cold, choking vapor. "Julie," she called, "Julie, where are you?"

"Here . . ." The always-assured Julie sounded very, very frightened. "I'm over here."

At last Rebecca spotted her through the fog. She lay on her back with her head raised. "My body . . . I can't—" Panic filled her voice. "Becka, I'm paralyzed. I can't move!"

The thought filled Becka with fear and rage. Julie was a gifted athlete. She was going to State in track. She lived and breathed sports. And there she was, lying on the floor, twisted in a heap. "Stop this!" Becka shouted to no one in particular. "I demand that you stop this! Stop these lies!"

As if in response, the floor started to rumble and shake again. But Becka would not back down. "In the name of Jesus Christ, I demand that you stop this! Now! Stop it this instant!"

The rumbling subsided. Slowly, until it had completely died. As it faded, the fog also began to dissolve. Not completely, but enough that Becka could make out the others scattered around the room.

There were Philip and Krissi huddled together on the floor. Beyond them she could see Scotty helping Darryl to his feet. And beside her was Julie—too strong to cry, but unable to move and wild-eyed with fear.

But where was Ryan? And what had happened to the Ascension Lady?

Becka knew what she had to do. As frightening as it was downstairs, she knew the source of the evil was upstairs. In the room at the end of the hall. The room where they had seen the shadows fighting. The room that had been videotaped. . . .

If they were going to put an end to this, they were going to have to confront whatever was in that room. And the only place to confront it was at its source.

Becka fought off a shiver. "OK," she said as she slowly rose to her feet. "Somebody give me a hand with Julie."

"Where . . . where are we going?" Philip asked timidly.

"We're going to stop this once and for all. We're going to get everyone back to normal." She sounded firm and in control on the outside. She just wished she felt that way inside.

It took all of Scott and Rebecca's encouragement and insistence, but the beleaguered troop finally rose to their feet and started forward. Becka nervously took the lead, followed by Julie, who was supported by Scott and Philip, and Darryl, who was led by Krissi.

Becka's face was firm with determination. This had to stop. Now.

~

9:10 P.M. "You look terrible," Todd said as he entered the church office.

Susan glanced up from her desk and instinctively straightened her hair. It was a mess. Though she and Todd had been married several months, she still always wanted to look her best around him.

"I brought Chinese," he said, referring to the large white sacks of food in his hands. The smell was wondrous, reminding Susan that she'd completely forgotten about dinner. He set the bags on the desk, gave her a kiss, and pulled up a seat. "So tell me what's going on."

"Rebecca Williams, her brother, and a bunch of friends are over at the Hawthorne Mansion."

"What are they doing there?"

"They're with Priscilla Bantini, the owner of the Ascension Bookshop. She's holding a séance."

Todd whistled softly. "We'd better get over there."

Susan shook her head. "No, I don't think so. I can't explain it, but I think . . . I think we're supposed to stay here. I think we'll be of more help staying here and fighting for them in prayer."

Todd looked at her a long moment. He really loved this lady. There was a quality about her, something so virtuous and connected to God that it made her more appealing than he'd ever dreamed a woman could be.

He smiled and pushed up his sleeves. "Then we'd better get down to business."

She nodded. They took one another's hands and bowed their heads. Susan glanced wistfully at the food sitting on her desk. It was going to be a while before they got to it.

✷

9:25 P.M. Rebecca and the group made their way into the entry hall. Just like before, there was the tinkling of crystal as the chandelier over their heads began swaying. And everyone went out of their way to avoid walking underneath it.

Now they stood before the massive stairway that loomed above them. As they paused, looking up, Scott joined Becka. "What do you think?"

"I think we don't have a choice."

Scott nodded silently.

"What was that?"

"I didn't hear—"

Becka held up her hand for quiet. There it was again. A faint whimpering. It came from under the stairway. "Who's there?" she called.

It stopped for a moment, then continued. Becka threw a look at Scott, then cautiously moved to investigate. "Who is it?" As she worked her way along the base of the stairs, she strained to see through the darkness. At last a shape came into view. It was the shape of a young man—one she knew very well— huddled against the wall.

"Ryan?"

The shape pulled itself closer to the wall, burying its face into its knees.

"Ryan?" She knelt and touched him. He looked up; his cheeks were stained with tears. It made her skin crawl. In all the time she had known him, she had never seen him cry. "Ryan . . . Ryan, what's wrong?"

His voice was thick. "They're dead!"

"What?"

"Mom, my sister, my little brother—" he swallowed back the rising emotion—"they're all . . . dead."

Becka's heart broke as she reached out for him. "No, Ryan, it's not true, it's a lie!" She pulled him close. He buried his face deep into her arms like a little boy. She held him tightly and could feel his body trembling with silent sobs. "It's all lies, Ryan, it's not true. None of it is true."

He looked up at her. Becka's throat ached with emotion as she stared down into those deep blue eyes. Eyes that usually sparkled with such life but were now filled with agony.

"I saw them," he choked. "I saw the crash." His lip started to tremble, but he fought to continue. "I was standing right there in the road, Beck. They swerved to miss me—I saw them hit . . . I saw them hit the truck."

"No, Ryan, it wasn't true, it was—"

"I saw!" He was shaking again, fighting back another sob. "I saw them go through the windshield . . . I saw my sister . . . her little head—" He broke off.

Becka's arms tightened around him. Tears burned her eyes as she stroked the back of his head, trying in vain to console him. At last she turned his face toward hers and looked directly into his swollen, red eyes. "Listen to me, Ryan. It's not true. It's a lie."

"But I saw it . . . I heard them screaming."

She shook her head. Tears spilled onto her own cheeks. "They're lies. That accident never happened."

He searched her face, trying to understand. She continued. "You can't go by what you see."

"But the screams—"

"You have to believe. Remember? We can't go by what we see or what we hear. We have to trust God, to believe what he says. His truth, Ryan, remember?"

New tears sprang to Ryan's eyes, only now they were tears of helplessness. "I can't," he croaked. "It's . . . too hard."

Becka swiped at her eyes. "I know. I know. But *he* can give you the faith. If you ask him, he'll give you the faith."

His eyes started to falter, to look away.

She gripped him tighter. "Ryan, God will help you believe!" She was practically shouting. "He'll help you believe, but you've got to ask, you've got to ask him!"

Her intensity drew his attention back to her. Then, ever so slowly, he began to nod. "Yes . . . ," he whispered.

Before Becka could respond, there was a sudden tumbling and crashing on the stairs above them. They scurried to their feet and ran to the base of the steps. Becka was the first to see him.

"Scotty!"

Her brother lay sprawled out at the bottom of the steps. He and the others had started to climb on their own, but he'd slipped and fallen. Yet it wasn't the falling that horrified Becka—it was her brother's neck. She had never seen a head twisted in such a strange position. Instantly, she knew the reason. His neck was broken.

"Scotty! Scotty, *no!!*" She dropped to his side. He did not respond. His eyes were closed and he was not breathing. "Scotty, Scotty, wake up! Scotty! Oh, God—no . . . please, please, not Scotty!" She threw her head back and cried. "Please, Jesus! Please."

Tears fell from her lashes onto his lifeless body. "I warned you!" she yelled. "I said you weren't protected. Dear God, please, please . . ."

"Becka—" Ryan knelt beside her. "This— this isn't true. It can't be."

"What are you talking about?" she wailed. "Look for yourself."

"No, no, it's just what you told me. This isn't real; this couldn't have happened."

"Look at him!" she shouted.

"It's not real, Beck." Ryan's voice was growing steadier. "It's another lie. He believes in Jesus; he's protected."

"No, that's just it—he wasn't protected. He wasn't wearing his—"

"God wouldn't let something like this happen, not the God I've been reading about. He wouldn't let this happen to one of his own. Not by that—" he motioned toward the top of the stairs—"that thing."

"But—"

"Believe . . . Becka. You said it yourself, you've got to believe. Don't go by what you see; go by what you know. God wouldn't let something like this happen. Not here, not like this."

She continued staring at her little brother. Next to Mom, this was her greatest love, the only family she had left.

"Believe," Ryan repeated. "It's another lie . . . it's not true, it's a lie."

Becka blinked. Slowly her eyes rose to meet Ryan's. Was it possible? Was this just another counterfeit?

She looked back down to the body. No! This could not be her brother. Whatever it was, it was not Scotty. Scott was not dead. He couldn't be dead. Scotty was alive, Scotty was—

"Beck. Hey, Beck."

It was her brother's voice. But it wasn't coming from the body. It was coming from . . .

She looked about, baffled.

"Up here." She turned to the landing at the top of the stairs. There was Scotty, standing with the others. She gasped and looked back to the body in front of her.

It was gone.

"Beck, are you OK?" She looked back up. He was leaning against the rail, bracing himself against the pain in his head. He motioned for her. "There's something up here you'd better see. Hurry."

She threw a look at Ryan. He gave a half-smile. Together they rose and raced up the stairs.

10

9:50 P.M.

hen Becka
arrived she threw her arms around her little
brother. "Oh, Scotty, Scotty, you're all right!"

"Hey, easy." He glanced at the others, a
little embarrassed. Still he let her hold him a
minute because she seemed to need it.
Come to think of it, he did, too. Finally he
pried her away.

"Scotty," she spoke quickly, "you've got to forgive the Ascension Lady. If you don't you could get hurt. This isn't a game. Not this time. You've got to believe me on this, you've got to forgive her, you've got—"

"Hey, I know, I know—"

"You don't understand, you've got to—"

"I *know*, Beck." She stopped to look at him, and he nodded. "I know." He motioned toward the open door at the end of the hallway. She slowly turned, then drew her hands to her mouth.

There, through the doorway, in the middle of the room, danced the Ascension Lady. Her arms and legs flew in all directions; there was no flow, no sense of rhythm . . . just maniacal bouncing and jerking. It was as if she had become a marionette whose arms and legs were attached to invisible strings yanked by an insane puppeteer. The only control she had was over her face. It was full of bewildered horror.

"She needs us, Beck," Scott said quietly. "She needs our help. God's help."

Without taking her eyes from the doorway, Rebecca nodded.

Scotty went on. "She and I may have our differences, but that . . . no person should have to go through that." He motioned to their friends huddled together. "Or any of this."

Rebecca turned to him. "So you forgive her?"

"You think I'd be willing to go in there and face that . . . *whatever* it is, to help her if I didn't?"

Becka nodded. "But your headache, what about your headache?"

He shrugged. "It's starting to go away, but it's sure taking its time about it."

Becka looked back to the room. "We have to go in there, don't we?"

"If we're going to help her. Yeah."

Becka swallowed. "Just you and me?"

Scott looked back to the pathetic group huddled a few feet away—Philip with his near-blank expression helping to hold up the paralyzed Julie, Krissi with her ravaged face, Darryl unable to see.

"I think so, kiddo," Scott said, meeting his sister's eyes. "Just you and me."

"And me," Ryan stated as he stepped forward. "I'll go in there with you."

Beck and Scotty exchanged looks. Finally Becka shook her head. "I appreciate the offer, Ryan, but, uh—"

"You think just because I'm not Christian I can't face that." He sounded hurt and a little defensive.

Scott tried to explain. "It's nothing against you, Ryan. It's just—if you go in there and you're not protected, if you don't have the authority of Christ . . . who knows what will happen. It just isn't smart."

"But you guys going in there by yourselves is?"

Becka knew he was trying to help, to protect her—and she loved him all the more for trying. "No." She shook her head. "That's the whole point. Scotty and I are not going in there by ourselves. We'll have help. We have God."

Ryan stared at her and slowly understood. He didn't like it, not one bit—but he understood. "Well . . . I'm right here. If anything goes wrong, if you need me, I'm right here."

Becka smiled. Then she rose up on her toes and kissed him softly on the cheek. "Thanks." They held each other's gaze a moment. Finally Becka turned back to face the room.

The wind had picked up again and was blowing against their faces.

"Well?" Scott asked.

Becka nodded. No more needed to be said. She held out her hand and he took it. They started forward. With each step they grew more and more nervous. Yet there was another part of them that grew more and more confident. They'd done this before. Well, sort of. And they'd definitely read about it. But was that enough?

"Know any good hymns?" Becka asked.

"That might not be a bad idea."

They continued to approach. "I'm waiting," she said.

After a moment Scott started to sing. "Jesus loves me, this I know. . . ."

Becka threw him a look.

"Hey, it's the best I can do on such short notice." He continued, "For the Bible tells me so . . ."

Becka took a deep breath and joined in. Her voice was weak and unsteady, and she felt more than a little foolish, but something was better than nothing.

"Little ones to him belong. They are weak, but he is strong."

They arrived at the door. The Ascension Lady looked helplessly at them. She was past exhaustion, and yet she continued the crazed dance. Wind whipped and howled around her so fiercely that Becka and Scott had to squint against it.

"Yes, Jesus loves me. Yes, Jesus loves me. Yes, Jesus loves me, the Bible tells me—"

Suddenly a voice began to chuckle, to reverberate throughout the room. But it wasn't one voice, it was several. They grew louder and louder. Mocking. Shrieking.

Becka covered her ears. "Stop it," she cried. "I command you to stop!"

The laughter decreased, but only slightly.

"Now!" Scott insisted. "We command you to stop, now!"

The laughter faded into the howling wind.

"And the Ascension Lady!" Scott shouted. "Release her! Now!"

There was no response. In fact, she seemed to leap and bounce even more violently.

"Now!" Becka shouted. "In the name of Jesus Christ, let her go, now!"

Instantly the woman crumpled to the ground in a heap.

Becka and Scott raced to her side. She groaned and stirred. But the ordeal had been too much, and she lapsed into unconsciousness.

Scott scanned the room. Other than the wind it was completely empty. "Where is she?"

"Who? Juanita?"

"Yeah, or whatever it is."

Becka looked about, shaking her head. Scott rose and took a step forward. "Where are you?" he shouted.

No response.

"We demand that you reveal yourself!"

At first neither of them saw a thing.

"In the name of Christ the Lord, we demand that you reveal yourself!" he repeated.

Slowly, faint outlines began to waver and shimmer all across the floor, filling the entire room.

"Are you seeing what I'm seeing?" Scott asked.

Becka nodded. "There's hundreds of them."

"No." He shook his head. "It's another trick." Raising his voice, he shouted, "In the name of Jesus Christ of Nazareth, I command you to stop your lies! I demand to see the truth."

But the images grew brighter, more solid. They averaged between two and three feet high. Their bodies were misshapen, some hunchbacked, some twisted and gnarled, most were covered with fur or hair. Their faces were equally grotesque: bulging eyes, pig snouts, gaping fangs, a few even had horns. Becka was struck by how much they looked like the pictures she'd seen of gargoyles on top of ancient buildings in Europe.

"We demand the truth," Scott repeated. "We demand to see you for who you are!"

The images grew even more solid.

"Scotty . . . maybe they are telling the truth. Maybe there is more than one."

The creatures stared at them, snarling, growling, snapping their teeth. Many began taking tentative, threatening steps toward them.

149

"Now what?" Scott asked.

Becka rose to her feet. The creatures continued closing in. But when Becka brushed the blowing hair from her eyes, the quick motion set the entire group scurrying backward.

Scott looked at Beck and raised his eyebrows.

When the creatures were convinced the threat had passed, they started toward them again. Suddenly, Scott made a quick movement of his own. Once again, they scurried backwards.

Scott shook his head, marveling. "It's a bluff. They want us to think they have power, but it's all a bluff. They're scared to death of us."

He turned on a group to his left. "Boo!"

The things jumped and fell over each other in their attempt to back up. Scott couldn't help laughing.

Becka saw no humor. "Scotty, this isn't a time to fool around."

He spun to the right. "Booga-booga!" Again they scurried backwards, but not quite as far or as fast. And their recovery was a lot quicker. They resumed closing in.

"Scotty . . ."

He paid no attention. This time he leaped forward. "ROARrrr . . ." But he stopped short as his foot tripped over the nearest creature, a hairy troll-like animal. Before Scott could catch himself, he stumbled forward, nearly caught his balance, then lost it again, falling headlong into the swarming mass of fur and claws.

They covered him instantly.

He screamed, but his voice was quickly muffled.

"Scotty!" Becka lunged for him, directly into the midst of the ghouls. She kicked them aside, slapping and hitting the ones trying to crawl up her legs. But there were too many. When she knocked one down, a dozen took its place. But she wouldn't stop.

The creatures latched onto her legs and started to swarm over her. Raw panic filled her mind.

"Scotty!" she screamed.

More and more reached up from the floor, grabbing her legs, trying to pull her down. She kicked and stomped. They tugged harder. She stumbled, began to lose her balance.

"Scot—"

She fought hard and kicked with all her might, but nothing helped.

They had her.

She tripped once, twice, then fell, plunging into the mass of swarming creatures.

They were all over her, smothering her, choking her, yet she managed to scream out, "In the name of Jesus, stop! I command you to stop!"

Instantly, there was only floor. No ghouls, no gargoyles, no furry monsters. Just hard oaken floor. The creatures . . . the demons were gone.

She groaned and rolled onto her side. Scotty was lying next to her. "Scotty." She reached out and shook him. "Scotty, wake up. We've got to get out of here."

He stirred slightly but remained unconscious. With great effort Becka forced herself to sit up.

And then she saw it—and her blood ran cold as a horrified scream froze in her throat.

11

10:00 P.M.

usan and
Todd had been interceding so intensely that
they had no idea of the time that had
passed. As they sat together, their prayers
came in different forms. Sometimes they just
offered earnest pleadings: "Dear God,
please, please . . ." Other times, they wor-
shiped quietly: "We love you, Lord; we adore

you." They also sang gentle songs and read sections of the Bible—and they took authority over Satan and bound and rebuked him.

But now, suddenly, they felt a strange peace. Instantly, they both knew everything would be all right, that it was all under control. Not because they knew what was happening at the mansion . . . but because of the presence. . . .

As they sat together, their eyes closed, they both knew there was something—some*one*—filling the small office. Neither Susan nor Todd heard a thing, nor did they open their eyes. They didn't have to. They just knew. And as the presence of God continued to flood the room, the peace continued to pour into their hearts. There was a power all around them. An indescribable power. Love. All-consuming love.

"Thank you, Jesus," Susan whispered. "Thank you, thank you . . ."

Todd nodded in agreement as tears slipped from his closed eyes.

Neither one knew how long they sat like that. It could have been a minute; it could have been hours. Time no longer seemed to exist. As the presence remained, a thought slowly took shape in Todd and Susan's minds. A command. They were to continue praying. Only now it was for something specific.

Susan was the first to put it into words: "Dear Lord, we ask you raise up others to pray. Right now. We pray that you would raise up other believers to intercede for our friends, to help them fight their battle. . . ."

~

10:03 P.M.

"Pull over."

"What?"

"Stop the car!" Mom Williams shouted across the seat to the driver. "We have to pull over."

"Now?" the driver, her oldest sister, asked.

"It's my kids. Something's wrong with Becka and Scotty. We've got to pray for them."

Mom's sister gave her a wary look. The afternoon funeral for their aunt had taken its toll on everyone's emotions. But Claire was the last person she thought would crack under the strain. After all, wasn't she the strong Christian in the family?

Mom saw the look on her sister's face and tried to explain. "Please, Sharon, don't ask me how I know. I just . . . I just know."

"We'll be home in ten minutes. Can't it wait?"

Mom thought for a moment, then slowly shook her head. "No." She peered out the windshield. "No, it can't. Look, there's a McDonald's up ahead. Pull into the parking lot and pray with me."

Sharon hesitated.

"Please, you've got to trust me on this."

Grudgingly, Sharon nodded and pulled into the parking lot. She'd barely turned off the ignition when her sister had reached out and taken her hands. A moment later, the two women had their heads bowed and were praying.

~

10:10 P.M. At the far end of the room—across from where Becka sat, exhausted, her hand resting protectively on Scott's unconscious form—the shadowy form of a little girl was taking shape. She was made up of the creatures. They had reappeared and were scurrying over to her, leaping into her, creating her very being, her substance. As each one entered her shadow, it became a part of her body, making her just a little larger.

Becka looked on in astonishment as the girl's height rose four, five, six feet. And still the creatures poured in. By the time the final ghoul had entered, the girl towered nearly ten feet tall, filling the bedroom from floor to ceiling.

Once her form was complete, she turned to Becka, who instantly recognized the face. It was Juanita. Instinctively, Becka pulled herself closer to Scotty, hoping somehow his presence would help.

It did not.

Juanita slowly raised her hand and pointed her finger directly at Rebecca. She spoke. Her voice thundered, low and guttural.

"YOU!"

Becka started to tremble. She was cowering in fear and she hated herself for it, but she had been through too much, seen too many things. She was exhausted.

The shadow smiled maliciously, then started to approach. It pointed to the Ascension Lady's body lying on the floor, then swept its hand to include Scotty's still form.

"THIS IS YOUR DOING."

Becka could not respond. She drew even closer to Scotty.

"ALL THIS SUFFERING—EVERYONE SUFFERS BECAUSE OF YOU."

Becka shook her head, trying not to listen. But the voice was powerful and persuasive, as were the creature's eyes. As she watched it approach, Becka found it more and more difficult to resist or look away.

"IT IS YOUR PRIDE, YOUR NARROW-MINDEDNESS THAT HAS CREATED THIS."

Becka tried to block the voice from her mind, but it had gotten inside. And the closer Juanita approached, the more it seemed to make sense.

"YOU THINK THERE IS ONLY ONE WAY. YOUR WAY! SUCH ARROGANCE HAS LED TO THIS SUFFERING."

Becka closed her eyes. Was this thing right? Was it really her fault? What would have happened if she'd listened to the Ascension Lady and helped from the beginning? She should have been open-minded, she should have been more willing to compromise. . . .

Her eyes started to burn with tears. It *was* her fault. When you got down to it, all of this was her doing.

"THERE ARE MANY WAYS TO THE LIGHT. YOUR STUBBORNNESS HAS BLOCKED THEM ALL."

Becka started to cry. Deep, heart-wrenching sobs shook her. The thing moved closer. Becka didn't have to open her eyes to feel it towering above her. But she no longer cared . . . she no longer had the energy or the will to fight. Whatever happened next was what she deserved. It was time to quit. Time to stop hurting others and give in.

The closer the thing bent toward her, the more she could feel her will and determination drain away. All she wanted was to sleep.

To stop fighting, to give in, to let the thing take control.

"YOU WILL NO LONGER RESIST. YOU WILL LEARN OTHER WAYS. YOU WILL—"

"She will not!" It was Ryan. His voice sounded far, far away, but Becka still heard it. "There are no other ways! Jesus said, 'I am the way and the truth and the life. No one comes to the Father except through me!'*"

The thing cried in surprise and staggered backward.

Becka felt her strength returning. Her eyes fluttered, then opened. Ryan stood inside the room. The shadow thing looked angry and confused, but when it spotted Ryan, its confusion gave way to mocking laughter.

"AND WHO ARE YOU TO OPPOSE US?"

Ryan swallowed hard and shouted. "I am Ryan Riordan."

"YOU HAVE NO AUTHORITY."

The boy was nervous, but he held his ground. "Of course I do. I am a Christian."

Becka's heart leaped to her throat. Was it possible?

"THAT GIVES YOU NO AUTHORITY."

Ryan hesitated, unsure. He threw a frightened look at Rebecca.

She looked on, still stunned. Then slowly a thought took shape. Maybe it was true.

Maybe Ryan couldn't face this thing. Any more than she could . . . not on their own. But with the two of them together, joining forces . . . joined in faith. . . . What was it the Bible said? "If two of you agree down here on earth concerning anything you ask for, my Father in heaven will do it for you."

She took a deep breath, then shouted, "You're a liar!"

The thing spun back to her. "HE HAS NO AUTHORITY."

Becka racked her brain, trying to remember more of the Bible verses she'd been learning. Another sprang to her mind, and she shouted, "'I have given you authority. . . . Whatever you bind on earth is bound in heaven.'"

The shadow cried and fell backward as if it had been hit.

Becka and Ryan exchanged looks across the room. They understood instantly. *This* was the sword they had talked about: the power of the Word of God. Ryan took a step closer and shouted: "'I am the way and the truth and the life. No one comes to the Father except through Me.'*"

Again the creature roared, part in anger, part in anguish. Rebecca threw a look to Ryan, puzzled that he'd chosen the same verse as before.

He shrugged. "It's the only one I know."

She almost smiled. With courage growing, she finally rose to her feet. They were finally on the offensive. Another verse came to mind. "'Resist the devil, and he will flee from you.'*"

More agonized shouts. The shadow thing started to back up toward the distant corner.

"THIS IS OUR DOMAIN. WE HAVE BEEN GRANTED IT."

"You're a liar," Becka shouted. "Everything you say is a lie. 'There is not an iota of truth in the devil. . . . He is the father of liars!'"

The creature roared.

"Stop it!" Becka cried. "Stop it this instant."

The shadow fell silent.

Still trembling, Becka forced herself to approach. "I demand that you stop these—"

"YOU HAVE NO AUTHORITY."

"'The Lord rebuke you!'*"

The creature shrieked, this time writhing as if someone had thrown acid on it. With growing confidence, Becka continued her approach. Ryan followed suit.

"I order you to stop these lies!"

"I AM NOT—"

Becka raised her hand for silence, and the creature obeyed.

"I order you to stop these lies. No more games, no more counterfeits."

"I WILL NOT. I WILL—"

"In the name of Jesus Christ, I command you to go!"

The creature glared in rage.

"Now!"

Suddenly a brilliant light exploded from the thing's very center. It was so intense that Becka and Ryan had to look away. It sparkled and crackled throughout the creature's body. The thing screamed in agony and the room roared with thunder that reverberated through the entire house. But as the light faded, so did the creature. In less than a second it was gone. Its tormented shrieks and thundering took a bit longer to fade as they echoed about the room, but they, too, finally disappeared.

Rebecca and Ryan looked around. Everything had returned to normal. No wind, no howling. Most importantly, no Juanita. It was over.

Julie stuck her head through the doorway. To Becka's relief she looked perfectly normal.

"Is everything OK?" she asked.

Becka nodded. Julie stepped inside, followed by the others. Each looked worn and rumpled, but the illusions were gone. Everyone was back to their original selves. Even the Ascension Lady had regained conscious-

ness and was sitting up, although she still
looked pretty dazed and confused.

Ryan eased a step toward the corner
where Juanita had last been. "Is she gone?
She is, isn't she?"

"No."

Becka turned around to see Scotty rising
to his feet. "She . . . they're still here," he
said. "I can feel them. They're just playing
possum."

Becka shuddered. Would this never end?
She watched as her brother crossed to her.
He reached down, took her hand, gave it a
squeeze, then lowered it gently to her side.
Without a word, he turned and walked
toward the corner.

"Scotty?"

He did not answer.

"Scotty!"

When he reached the corner, he turned
back to Becka and tried to flash her that lop-
sided grin of his. He didn't quite pull it off.

Becka watched as he turned back to the
corner. He took a deep breath, hesitated,
then said in a loud, controlled voice: "By the
power and authority of Jesus Christ of Nazareth, I cast all of you out of this house and
into the abyss!"

Nothing happened. There was no
response. The room was as silent as ever.

Scott cleared his throat and took another
breath. "I command you to obey me . . . now!"

A faint breeze began to stir.

Everyone exchanged looks.

The breeze increased, blowing their hair.
Soon it was tugging at their clothes, whip-
ping their jackets. The moaning returned,
growing louder and louder as the wind
turned into a full-fledged gale. The moans
evolved to wailing, then shrieks. The group
bent down, some hanging onto one
another—anything to keep their balance.

Scott was the first to see it. A slit of light in
the corner directly before him. It was no
longer than a foot and only a couple inches
wide. The wind raced into it. Faster and
faster the air roared past Scott and into the
hole, until Scott himself started to be pulled
in.

"Scotty!"

His footing slipped once, twice. He was los-
ing his balance, being sucked into the opening. He tried to fight it, to pull back, but the
force was too great.

Becka raced to his side, grabbing his arm,
pulling for all she was worth. Ryan joined
her and pulled the other arm. Together they
hung on, refusing to let go. It seemed to last
forever, though it was probably only a few
seconds. Finally the wind died and, as the

last of it disappeared, rushing into the opening, the slit of light vanished as well.

The wind was gone. Everything was still. Only the heavy breathing of Becka, Scott, and Ryan broke the silence.

Scott looked to Becka, then to Ryan, who was flipping the hair out of his eyes. They traded grins. It was over. For real this time. They were sure of it. Becka was the first to hold out her arms. The two guys instantly responded, and they fell into a three-way hug, each holding the others for all they were worth.

The others joined in—Julie, Philip, Krissi, Darryl . . . even the Ascension Lady. She had stood off to the side, watching, until they motioned for her to join them. Everyone held everyone else in a massive group hug. It had been quite a night. It had been quite a seventy-two hours!

Of course, it wasn't entirely over. Both Becka and Scott knew there would be plenty of questions to be asked and explanations to be made. But one thing was certain: The Bible could be trusted. Always.

It said there were not ghosts, only Satan and his fallen angels.

It was right.

It said Christians had authority through Christ to beat them.

Right again.

All they had to do was take that authority, use the sword of God's Word, and wear God's armor—*all* of it, including the breastplate of righteousness.

Becka and Scott weren't fools. They knew they didn't have to be perfect to face the enemy—they just had to be headed in that direction. And when they messed up, they had to make sure they admitted it and asked Christ to forgive them.

All of these were important lessons they'd learned. Lessons that would help them in upcoming battles. Not that they'd go looking for fights with Satan and his groupies. They knew better than that. But they knew if and when they were called to help, they would go into battle, willing to fight and, with God's help, to win. That was a part of being warriors for the Lord.

Only now there were not just two warriors. Becka looked at Ryan and gave him an extra-hard hug. He flashed her that killer smile, the one that always made her stomach do flip-flops, and she smiled back.

Now there were three.

AUTHOR'S NOTE

As I continue writing this series, I have two equal and opposing concerns. First, I don't want the reader to be too frightened of the devil. Compared to Jesus Christ, Satan is a wimp. The two aren't even in the same league. Although the supernatural evil in these books is based on a certain amount of fact, it's important to understand the awesome protection Jesus Christ offers to all those who have committed their lives to him.

This brings me to my second and somewhat opposing concern: Although the powers of darkness are nothing compared to the power of Jesus Christ and the authority he has given his followers, spiritual warfare is not something we casually stroll into. The situations in these novels are extreme to create suspense and drama. But if you should find yourself involved in something even vaguely similar, don't confront it alone. Find an older, more mature Christian (such as a parent, pastor, or youth leader) to talk to. Let them check the situation out to see what is happening, and ask them to help you deal with it.

Yes, we have the victory through Christ, but we should never send in inexperienced soldiers to fight the battle.

Oh, and one final note. When this series was conceived, there were really no bad guys on the Internet. Unfortunately that has changed. Today there are plenty of people out there trying to draw young folks into dangerous situations through it. Although the characters in this series trust Z, if you should run into a similar situation, be smart. Anyone can *sound* kind and understanding, but their intentions may be entirely different. All that to say, don't take candy from strangers you see . . . or trust those you don't.

Bill

END NOTES

Chapter 2
2:04 P.M.
"We are confident, I say, and would prefer to be away from the body and at home with the Lord." (2 Corinthians 5:8, NIV)

"It is destined that men die only once, and after that comes judgment." (Hebrews 9:27a)

Chapter 3
11:54 P.M.
Information on astrology taken from *Hot Topics, Tough Questions* by Bill Myers (Wheaton, Ill.: Victor Books, 1987) 96–97.

Chapter 4
7:10 P.M.
"Jesus had commanded the evil spirit to come out of the man. . . . Jesus asked [the demon], 'What is your name?' 'Legion,' he replied, because many demons had gone into him. And they begged him repeatedly not to order them to go into the Abyss." (Luke 8:29-31, NIV)

"I have given you authority over all the power of the Enemy." (Luke 10:19)

"Whatever you bind on earth is bound in heaven." (Matthew 18:18)

"There is not an iota of truth in him. When he lies, it is perfectly normal; for he is the father of liars." (John 8:44)

"If two of you agree down here on earth concerning anything you ask for, my Father in heaven will do it for you." (Matthew 18:19)

Chapter 10
10:20 P.M.
"I am the way and the truth and the life. No one comes to the Father except through me!" (John 14:6, NIV)

"Resist the devil, and he will flee from you." (James 4:7, NIV)

"The Lord rebuke you!" (Jude 1:9, NIV)